THE UNEARTHING OF THE MAYANS' SEEDS
The Last Inscription

Kamow Buchanan

authorHOUSE®

AuthorHouse™
1663 Liberty Drive
Bloomington, IN 47403
www.authorhouse.com
Phone: 1-800-839-8640

Published by AuthorHouse   7/18/2012
ISBN: 978-1-4772-4508-8 (sc)
ISBN: 978-1-4772-4510-1 (dj)
ISBN: 978-1-4772-4509-5 (e)

Library of Congress Control Number: 2012912621

First and foremost, before the story begins— I would like to take this time, to recognize the ability through which I was able to paint this story; with my foresights and mental brushes. I am truly glad as elated that I did not take this gift for granted.

Whether I sell one book or a million, I am gratefully humbled that I've completed a task that came to me from one tiny vision; to a full manuscript.

 I would like to acknowledge my closest confidants and care givers, those who have wanted nothing but the best for me: Mr. Gray| Mrs. Mann/punk| Lona Minto| the Minto's/Sylvan & Paulette Minto| K. Brown| Mr. Nembhard| the Buchanan's| Jaide & Alexia, daddy will always love you…

If I failed to mention your name, this book is a reminder in a reward; that from your planting, instilling and investing in me; you should be proud of this reaping…

Contact info: superstar-m@hotmail.com
Twitter: @djusha
Facebook: @Kamow Buchanan

Somewhere beyond the forefronts of ancient times; a place that as only been buried in our unsound minds, somewhere-far-fetch from this current time and destination, a domain that measure deeper than ocean floor to bluest skies, yet shallow enough to have been deciphered; this story was left in the entanglement of a dreamers woven nets; a group of gifted individuals once had gathered around a pile of burning wood, the scent of ancient-incents mystified the aura and complimented the-tales of the mood that lasted until the spirits of the candles had gone from liquid to a solid state and the woods of the out-bushes went from axed to ashes.   Concocted potions of magic, medicines as well as the unknown are all around the room, the silent chants of our Mayan people evoked the glow of the promising moons, yet the sounds of the furry hoofing jackasses stuttering; rumbled out of the stables roof. Feathers of many kinds are standing up right in the circumference of the inscribers' ink-jar; ready to redeem and relay the messages and anomalies that are yet to happen.

The chief Mayan elder, sat at the top of the table in a trance of redeem and magical focus while his ambassadors of spiritual-receivers, transcribers and travelers sat on the opposite sides of the old-wooden-table; he spoke wisdoms that carried courage's, divine-intellect as well as unanswered questions»» far beyond the distance of hope.

If one thing was as persuaded; the Mayan people were not that curious about their own Endeavour's, simply because they knew their places in history, their purposes and their ultimate-cause of prize, pride and price. When all is said and done and our people have long-since vanished from the face of this earth, what will mankind have learned, would they have received the messages we've written, what will be the outcome of our story, beyond the distant rivers, mountains and circling seas?

One inscriber implies that one thing will remain as persuaded; our footprints will forever be stamped and remain buried into the village-shore as a reminder of our given gifts, which will remain secretly seeded until planted by the hands of the chosen.

CHAPTER 1

A-thousand-one-hundred-and-seventy-four-miles in the Northern direction from this estrange position at which the picture plays like a child, in the garden of tender protection, the crystallite and snowploughs demonstrates their intangibility, while the salt trucks frantically tries to reverse the coagulation of the city's streets; somehow in many ways than one, life is graciously adapted naturally in this frigid location. The steams from a-top neighbouring chimneys, factory's and exhaust-pipes, arises with the combustive-intentions to evaporate into the smog filled recession; above the greyish-florescent-dense-atmospheric-skies, which hovers around a place where; the squirrels, the blue-jays and the beavers, plus: millions of strong, brave, daring, kind, helpful and willing individuals recite to call this daunting place their very home.

In each household from nearest to farthest, the inscription clearly depicts; mankind has surpassed the rules of each pharaoh and written prophesies from ancient past to today's booming 21first century. But the written knowledge of the greatest believers and foreseers is yet to be spoken; as it was once written and color-coded into the homage of the inscribers scroll.

Mr. & Mrs. *Dubwise* neatly put their vacationers' luggage-sets into a chartered limo before they set off to encounter Paradise and limitless romance at the hands of doctorate-degree that Mr. *Dubwises'* money does buy.

But out in the backyard, a furry-gluttonous-hoof, chews up the remnant sardine-can that was left in the garbage disposal.

Just around the corner from where the furry-gluttonous-hoof of a jackass chews and then swallows, the smell of sugarcane stains the surrounding atmospheres' as the steams and stench pushes across the blue backdrop as the local distillery over-proofed potions settles then brews; it traveled up to the mist of the solid mountain range then disguise itself with the guardians of **wealth**.

As this afternoon switches from sunlight to sunset, the sounds of our roosters, fade drastically as the **golden** hen, settles into the kingdom of the roosters' ruse; but as some may call this epic tale as is, (**pheasantly**) hen and rooster settles in the love nest.

The livelihood of the insects twitching, chirping and chime-like distinctive melodies; serenaded the sunlight as it rested behind the camouflage of the closing dark element we prescribed as night fall.

Unlike the clever dragonfly, the firefly illuminates its presence in total undisguised of its natural, nightly flight.

But inside this humble home of mine»» our television transpires all pictures in black-&-white; with often distortional weaving grains that twitches our eyes… but nonetheless, a tranquility-like magic energize each life; instilling enthusiasm in all of our prides.

Naturally, we begin to fade into the hands of relaxation… graciously we all settle in bed to rest and play in our dreams and some may dismay the fact that the sound of the supernatural prowls high in the surrounding mountains, in our backyards, valleys and streets, rivers as well as the circling seas. As importantly, the sounds of our guard-dogs, identifies whenever they detected the steps of trolling feet...

We remunerate honourably at the sight and sound of a new day.

When the sun came up across the distant horizon; it brought along excitement, festivities and betters hope; pride in the people as well as the unseen drifters; the guilt's and secrets of the past, the noble ones as well as the heartless rulers and them who were chosen.

Today the enthusiasm in and around the village was greatly amplified by the sounds of stability, strength and supporters who cheered on the practicing hoofs; Just as it was accruing many centuries ago. In addition, they could not escape the shame that was swept up under the grass; as the scars of the haunting past stood consciously in their hearts.

The spoken tales in the village was that; there were three unseen, transparent, eyewitnesses in the stands among the living-livelihood of the festivities; who stunk like the potion from our national brewery.

Mr. and Mrs. *Dubwise*, applies considerable amounts of sun block before they charted their way aboard the company's tour bus, followed by the driver and decorative tours guide.

All the other sun-blocked patrons,' settled in the air-conditioned bus, with their expensive sandals and sunshades; perkily in place as the tour bus smokes off up the contouring valleys.

As the tours guide explains: patrons clapped, danced and cheered to finally be off in paradise; for a small price at sightseeing. As the tour bus powered on by; all who were aboard the air-conditioned friendly zone, rushed to the left side of the village wagon to catch a glimpse of the festivities that was happening on by.

The decorative tours guide announces; "that today was the national jackass derby, where stakes are high and losers are more likely to wear the jackasses crown for the rest of their given donkey lives..." He spoke; "that today was a noble deed in the respects of where the furry hoofing racers had come from." "Where did they come from?" asked a few curious individual whose identity lay hidden underneath the big straw hats and expensive sun shades. "From the cargo-bay of the strangers' ship" replied the decorative tour guide; with a deep sense of mysteriousness yet conveying respects imbedded in his voice.

Approximately: 27.7 nautical miles in the west direction from the very location where the furry-gluttonous-hoofing-jackass dismantles the sardine can; seven year-old *Mustave* dines on a combination of: sardines, string-beans and grounded wheat.

After he finishes his afternoon's container of carbohydrates, iron, energy and protein; *Mustave,* rinses his **gold**-pin-striped-plate at the pipe that stood at the near side to his two-bedroom-house.

Mustave rushes off in the distant; to settle the scores with the other village kids as they practice their savvy techniques, skills and rivalry at a serious game of marbles.

Before the atmosphere began cascading darkness upon the village, *Mustave,* hurries back to his yard with his hand and pocket full of marbles, which he won from the others. *It was clear that Mustave, was a selective-articulate-destined-winner; who did not fear the stakes of any gamble but was always the one to walk away with his ethics;* **Worthing its weight in gold.**

Mustave then hid his marbles and his **golden-glory** out in the backyard before he stepped inside. When he settles in the house; *Mustave* climbs up on to his home-made bench, in front of is golden television, where the pictures translate in black and white.

Mustave is granted with this opportunity in the ammonites of the television, to familiarize his mentality in the black and the whiter sides of life: in the black and the white that projects in his television. But the odd new was; none of it all mattered or made a slight bit of sense because the clarity of the picture stayed the very same each time Mustave rushes in the house, to summarize life in black and white.

Impatiently, a passing playful breeze spun the receiving antenna out of reception; that causes a negative reaction to the television, which makes distortional like grains; which then destroys the picture of black and white.

Mustave then gets up from off his home-made bench and went into his bed at this night's intermission… but before the rooster begins to interpolate the environment with its negative annoying calls; Mustave is long since out in the back yard with a bucket of water and a hand full of salt -- not to mention a generous amount of excitement for what Edith was preparing in the kitchen for share.

Depressingly so, Mustave attends to his four hoofed transportation as he scraped away the remaining dried sleep form the surfaces of his eyes.

Two mornings before this prior intervention, Mustaves' mother; readies his khaki attire with repeated seams and pleats from top to bottom on his tops and bottoms; with an *ancient-raw-hot-casted-steel-iron* that sat on a pot of red hot coals.

When Mustave was certain his transportation was finally satisfied and happily tentative, he hurried back to the smell of fried-fish and fresh hard-dough-bread that were crisping away on the hot pot of crackling coals.

Not too long after Mustave was neatly in his seamed uniform; boasting pleats, pockets and unique epaulettes on both shoulders... His mother packed his lunchbox, kissed him goodbye and gave him words of advises before he led his transportation through the stables gate.

Mustave was a dapper to the testament of: sharp, diligent and impressively-well dressed when he left out the house; clean and clear as a referee's whistle. But when he came through the school yard gates, his attire was rumpled out of his mother's perfection, in addition, soiled with many hoof imprints as well as coated with fur. It was as if Mustave was caught between cap and trading fur, someplace between his home and out in the felids on route to school.

It must have been that Mustave was having many difficulties with his stubborn transportation. Mustave was not in dismay of the condition of his attire, more so retired and tired of the constant abuse of the others who; spoke, mocked and jeered disregards at his transportation, which was a blatant shadow to his reputation.

Nonetheless, Mustave hid his stresses and kept a focus check on the clock and his lunchbox and lunch break recession. All the other children in the classroom knew exactly what would transpire at today's lunch recession; as if it was the leading lesson of their daily provisions.

Just before the lunch bell sounds, all the student in class taunts and laughed distressingly when they noticed Mustave's transportation chewing on its rope.

All but one boy was intrigued by the simulations of Mustaves' daily pouts, demises and harden gloats and this boy and Mustave would share many things in common... but as the lunch bell sounds; a true friendship is left in the open for speculations between: Mustave and Kyro.

Mustave and all the others; gather their belongings with lunchboxes in hand and make way to the canteen, where Mustave extracts his lunchbox and started to unmask such items that his mother had prepared for share.

Bounded in between brown paper-bag, in addition, tied up in black plastic scandals Mustave reveals:

2 mangoes

2 bananas

2 slices of pudding

2 fried-fishes

1 jar of sweet lemonade and 4 slice of hard-dough-bread.

By the time lunch break is near over, Mustave is sound asleep; sounding as though he was a trailer hauling logs through the forest... however, when he finally snaps out of his comatose state/mid day's nap, Mustave faces a sadder reality that classes are over, school is closed, the students and teacher had somehow disappeared in absolute silence. But the sadder part is that; Konrad has left building with benighted inexcusability on all hoofing-4-cylinders.

On that note, well rested with energy to burn, Mustave covered his lemonade jar and prepare to journey home to his distant village; on all 2 cylinders as the smell of fish, fruits and lemonade-juices; subdued as it greatly lingers in the atmospheres'.

With each step taken on this time and thought-filled journey to his village, Mustave cannot come or bring justice as to why Konrad has chosen to do this time and time again.

Mustave was humiliated-- but he kept his emotions at the bottom of his lemonade jar.

As he continued covering grounds on his journey through the village, he becomes closer to his home...leaving his negative scepticism behind him in the distant far.

As Mustave closes-in on his village, he wonders if and when changes were of the essence? He was nearly out of empathy and patients with Konrads' selfish behaviours and he knew that his family would need to arrange alternate transportation—because; this was not the second or seventh time Konrad has pulled himself out of his knotted ropes and then out of the rabbit's hat and then disappeared. Not to mention, this was no longer the 18th century; things and time had been modernized for: (post) Stone Age sake.

As Mustave comes around the path that led across the ditch, he spots Konrad underneath the massive mango tree, out in the back yard sound asleep...

For over 5 years; Mustaves' mother had packed his lunch along with a separate portion for Konrad as well. As each day's recession comes around, Konrad would watch as Mustave devours his portion of fish, pudding, mangoes, banana and hard-dough-bread...not to mention his fair amount of sugar-doused-lemonade. As Konrad sulked in his unfair share of humiliations; Mustave falls in bellyful sleep. This is usually when Konrad kisses-his-teethes and begin his leave of absence!

Yet again, Mustaves' transportation has left the building, leaving all the students historically giggling.

Mustave's *jackass* was an embarrassment to his reputation; but a vital part in his life's transportation and his future, present and past educations.

Needless to say, there were no compromises of constituencies in the family's budget for any other form of transportation for Mustave. In their eyes and wise judgments; Konrad was the only exception and nothing else.

Mustaves' family told him that Konrad simply wanted respect and thoughtful communication; likewise magic of the wise and maybe a small portion of what was packed for share.

Mustave could not pin-point the moral of this recurring event. He did not understand the ethics of Konrads' embarrassments. However, there was injustice but equal amounts to be shared amongst the two, in this unselfish story.

When Mustave steps in his yard after a weary journey home from school, he is greeted with the smell of: fried-fish and fresh hard-dough-bread, in addition, a warm and tender hug from his mother Edith. Mustave immediately tells of his embarrassment and Konrads' selfish annulment acts. His mother handed him a hot fish to ease his hurts.

Once again it seems that Konrad politely evaded the tattletale hook of Mustave; who took pride in the hot fish that he was recently given.

Konrad was Mustaves' transportation Mondays through Fridays and shared the duty of Mustaves' grandfathers farming consumptions on the weekend.

For Konrad, it was to school and back, then up the hills of the side of the mountain where Mustaves' family had foreseen acres of farmlands.

For many years, this was all that Konrad has known. His ropes combined with rocky roads, Hamper, grass-saddle and straps has not yet taken their tolls.

Konrad was young stubborn and healthily pruned to carry a load; but for some strange reason has yet to carry Mustave through his village home from school where he usually leaves him in a comatose zone.

CHAPTER 2

"Thank god it is Friday evening; at least I could rest my legs and humility… Nonetheless, the tattletale and negative moans of Konrads' stubborn ways!" said Mustave.

"Heee-onnn, heee-onnn" replied Konrad; who reciprocated the mutual feeling of unselfishness and his story of full-grown governing laziness. In other words, what Konrd was trying to say is; learn to share you endless pit.

However, in the morning it was work as usual; as Mustave, his grandfather Mr. Levi and Konrad saddled up to journey up the mountain; to weed and fertilize the crop-beds, in the eye of their guardians.

With amicable movements in the kitchen, Edith works up a storm of fried-fish and fresh hard-dough-bread; so that lunch would be in the hamper when the boys were ready to break after the mornings weeding.

Mr. Levi cautiously covers his day's amount of freshly brewed pepper-mint-tea. He gathers his gardening utilities and stashed it all neatly inside Konrads' Hamper; just the way farmers are suppose to do; with dignity and pride.

Before the boys begin the journey up the mountain, Mustave attends to his transportation with a bucket of water and a hand full of sea-salt. In addition, his fair shares of inquisitions as to "*why Konrad was so god dam stubborn and lazy.*"

Even though Konrad kept his head buried in the bucket, he kept his undivided attention; with eyes and ears in the kitchen, where Edith was packing fair shares in Mustaves' lunch-box, in this natural order:

2 mangoes

2 bananas

2 slices of pudding

2 fried-fishes

4 slices of hard-dough-bread and the regular sugar-doused-Lemonade!

Naturally, Edith gave Mustave plenty kisses and hugs as mother are supposed to. Konrad expressively mumbles something in an ass's language before they took off. At approximately 5:35 am; the three strolls up the mountain. The sound of hoofs echoes as if an army had released a thousand troops, but as we already know or you mightn't have; it was Konrads' stability, combined with Edith's giving dignity that had his mind and nostrils in the lunch-box; he simply could not wait to get to the farming grounds and for lunch break to come flying around.

Konrad was eager but bitter about not getting his fair shares. Anyhow, it was just another Saturday morning, same selfish routine; as Konrad commuted his locomotive end of the deal.

Several years before Mr. Levi had acquired his many acres of farm-lands up in the mountain, something had happened that caused him to *change position in careers*. In addition, broaden his orison of superficial beliefs. He was at loss---- and stuck with harden compulsive thoughts with himself; that he should have believed the inscription of the messengers from three generations ago...but he was not the one to be blamed. He felt this misery anyhow.

Mr. Levi had taking his lifesaving, pension plan and redundant funds from his insurance return and purchased as many acres up the mountain as his combined monies would equal in square-footage. In addition, the blinding large amount of mist, massive trees and progressive eye-sore-boulders were a part of his title ownership.

At that moment in time; land up the mountain was very cheap! Which meant; *almost the entire mountain belonged to the Levi's family. In addition, justifies that Mustave was the sole proprietor and only beneficiary; in case Mr. Levi was or had kicked the life-less empty bucket from off mount-7; incarnating himself and gardening utilities.*

While others were purchasing lands closer to rivers and surrounding sea, destiny combine with fate and tragedy would lead Mr. Levi to hold the largest land-title of the village; that stated all but 2% of mount-7 belonged to the Levi's.

Mr. Levi was patiently humble but very aesthetic, a noble man; he believed in hard work, justice and giving and receiving. Even though Mr. Levi owned mount-7, it was for all the villagers to do as they'd wished. As long as they showed respect and gave a helping hand in his crop beds; in addition, cared for mount-7 as though it was their very own, Mr. Levi did not have any convulsions with that.

Each and every Saturday mornings at approximately 5:35 am, in the shadows of dark and presence of the rising sun, love and heartaches', emptiness and despairs would drive Mr. Levi up the mountain, with his troop: Konrad and Mustave, gardening utility, beverages and synthetic lunch-boxes as well peace of mind.

In addition, something that was dear to his heart was also pulling him to and from the grounds of mount-7. He was In search of his pride that barely-bared in the tilled crop-beds.

Mr. Levi was searching to find something that he had lost; in the sense of committing himself on his farm, up the hills of mount-7; he hoped that time and hard work would reward his loss.

Mr. Levi kept his focus-intrusive-attention on Mustave, as he sees the very reflection of what he'd lost and what he was searching to find... But he knew that time was passing by and he was getting much older; thus closer to demise, each time the troops hoofed up the side of the mountain. Mr. Levi knew that one day soon he would have to confess and put this delusional searching at rest-- before he was readily willing to be laid to rest himself.

As this day draws to a halt, Mr. Levi taps horrendously as many times as he could count on the shoulder of Mustave, to retrieve him from his lunch break hangover of: fried-fish and hard-dough-bread combined with pudding, mangoes, bananas and sugar- doused-lemonade. Konrad is seen sulking bitterly at Mustave who had not one ounce of consideration in mind or heart. Poor young Konrad settles belligerently on a patch of hay.

Immoderately, Konrads' hampers overloads with equipments and food that Mr. Levi had retrieved from his crop-beds and fruit trees. Like a careless summers breeze they make their way down the mountain without effort at moderate ease.

CHAPTER 3

Mr. and Mrs. Dubwise, has taken many timeless romantic vacations in the land of this delighted unbelievable place called Paradise and they both decided that it was time they summed up a positive conclusion; that this is where they would spend the rest of their natural life.

They had been many places in their lives and there was no place that felt more like home than the conspired village of asses and caring people, festivities and magic.

On their last romantic winters vacation, the two were very interested in a noble piece of the village land, where they fell in love with the festive jackasses derby and the surroundings beauty; plus golden peace of mind. In addition, that compassion that came from the mists of mount-7 had seeped into their souls and settled with a lasting impression.

Mrs. Dubwise was a retired veterinarian and has decided that her knowledge and inner compassion for animals; would do a lot of good, in training and caring for a few lucky hoofs that she was planning to enter into the asses' race at the annual derby.

Mr. Dubwise was a physician-practitioner/surgeon, doctor/retired scientist in the fields of pharmaceutical breakthroughs and remedies.

Moreover, he knew that his ambitious portfolio and skilled physician's background would be a rewarding asset to the country and neighbouring community.

More or less, it was time to give back to a much needed society and this was the place to generously do so. In addition, it was as if this was a positive-natural-calling for the Dub-wise's.

When they came to the village on this trip; they were prepared to settle there once and for all. Dressed as a true professional, Mr. Dubwise slams his briefcase on the table...pow!... confidently to show that he was ready to sign his deeds and land titles... so they could immediately begin construction on a 5 bed-room-mansion for the two, with a magnificent stable for the lucky few.

He opens his briefcase to expose stacked American $1000 bills. He takes out a pen and began to sign his life away. He then hands the briefcase over to the justice of land services and storms out the office with title and glory; to be the newest owner and neighbour in the pride driven village.

Edith was on her way to a nearby shop, she witnessed the two pail-pigment individual's glorious gloat as they happily waved on by. They mannerly stopped Edith and introduced themselves as Mr. and Mrs. Dubwise. "Good day to you" said Edith, "welcome to our village." Both Mr. and Mrs. Dubwise replied "our village is right!"

"I must inform you Edith, that we have decided to call"...as they blissfully both points in the direction; where he had just bought some acres... "Soon we will settle here until the last of our days." said the Dubwises'.

"We must admit, we fell in love with the village and decided that we would return once and final; to make it our new and welcoming home."

Edith nodded with a friendly smile as the brief but consistent conversation came to the end. They were seen heading off in separate direction.

CHAPTER 4

about 350 years ago; long before Mustave, Konrad and Kyro; far beyond the times of Edith and Mr. Levi; long before the village had planned and carried out the very first festive jackasses derby; back when the slave masters tossed his whip around the back of a stubborn slave; a few stubborn donkey stood on all four, in a digestive patch of golden hay; prayed upon by the mysterious Mayan-healers, inscribers, dreamers and visionaries.

7 Mayan individuals conspired their theories and in-scripted their calendars at a particular event; on a precise-premeditated-time; on a particular day on this very location.

It was said that crashing of the docks will divert the flocks, destroy farmers' crops as well as misplace the treasure box, in addition, bury the innocent upon the *golden* soils.

As the Mayans continued to chart this event of foreseen history, the inscriber draws a large sail on top of a deserted mountain. It was carried many distant nautical miles by a dynamic swell/vigorous-atomic-rough-wave. However, another entity inscribed that it was the hands of the burning bush. The inscribers hurriedly colors underneath the earth with his *golden* pigments; when this foreseen meditation was over, the chief sends his messengers along with the inscription: to a distant village, many nautical miles across Open-Ocean; to pre-warn of these catastrophic anomalies that was written in the charts of the stars.

Along with the messengers went an important inscription; healing herbs, plant seeds, gratitude, condolences and a pair of the best jackasses that was at the Mayans possessions.

He also sent along his love and regards with promises of untold wealth and a message for the Levi's family.

3 of the Mayans best sailor's, navigators and philanthropist among the list of things they could do— just to name a few; set off on this journey to fulfill the honour of the chiefs duty, with unprecedented amount of dignity and gratitude-held-respects.

Many members of the Mayans tribe carried the boxes that the chief had prescribed upon this distant village; meticulously to the river bank that journeyed out to open seas. In a single file formation and order they marched and chanted songs of Mayans codes; to discard: evil-power, bad happenings and to discard the harming of haunting as well as ghostly apparitions. They marched with a strong sense of superficial beliefs to a waiting boat, which swayed side to side in the strong movement of the currents; as if it was impatient to get on with this journey.

The chief waited at the drifting of the river banks– with his inscribed scroll and potions of ancient magic; well wishes, safe travels, safe returns and the secret of the sailor's scope that included the Mayans charts.

All the women from the tribe brought gifts; fried-fish, pudding, lemonade, fruits and vegetables as well as flask of liquor; herbal tea and a year's supply of hard-dough-bread. In addition, grains, wheat's and the intricate details of recipes as well the blueprint of how to create iron form stones.

It was a Mayans farewell nonetheless at the edge of the riverbank... the noble sailors waived as the boat drifted away beyond the Mayans distance; drifting into the unknown of open seas– *yet their endeavour carried promises of Mayan preservation inside each grain and dried seeds.* Effortlessly without fear, they were un-reluctant to honour their duty and utmost deeds; as requested by their elder chief.

It was said that the Mayans, profoundly believed in the foreseen events of catastrophic astrology– in which they received from their chanting, spiritual ancient meditation and manifestations. This myth was once and for all proven– by many Scientologists; that studied archives and artefacts that were found in and on the Mayans reservations and discovered inscriptions in the 21-firsts century.

On one particular inscription that was discovered in the chief's camp, its translation depicted»» the Mayans reliving foreseen events time and time again.

The three noble sailors that went to deliver the prospects of the chief's wishes knew what to expect out on the open ocean. As their vessel drifts onwards, they drank of the magical potion and chanted the secret ancient codes of strength and power.

As the night drew rapidly closer over their light, one sailor sparks up a sailor's lantern as well as the sailor's pipe and congested medicinal herbs to further amortize in the Mayans traditions.

Even though the three noble sailors premeditated the battled fight of foreseen sight with Mother Nature, they kept an itinerary on the prize of fulfilling the distant journey with pride and Mayans persistence. They then tend to the two young jackasses; who slept away at the drifting night on a box of magical Mayans hay.

One sailor rests his arm on the treasured filled boxes that contained tokens of the Mayans world. In addition, the inscriptions of the Mayans scroll.

At last— the sun had faded into the hand of the waiting darkness; where the stars told of everlasting scars; that were also encrypted into the Mayans charts and hearts.

It has been many hours since the vessel drifted from the edge of the riverbanks into open seas and I must say that transition was made with effortless ease, which meant the Water-Gods slept upon the steady seas.

Filled with purification of the Mayans pipe, the three sailors decide to finalize with a hard-earned bite.

Before they consumed the labours of the Mayans best homemade appetizers and delicacy, they prayed on the containers that were presented by the women in tribe.

At the sound of a-men; they began their fair-shares of filling bites!

The two jackasses that were soundly asleep– got up at the sound and smells of the friendly feast of fried-fishes and stomping of teeth; with curiosity nudged between their tongue and feet. Needless to say, this was not a feast for the glutton hoofs but a dearly reminder that when the sun came across the gleaming backdrop of the open seas, land and civilization would be at the villages peace.

One by one, the three noble sailors took their turns digesting a noble nap of sleep and it was down to sailor number three; to consolidate his amount of peace. He placed his head just on the asses grass and compacted straws, to consolidate his rest on pause— in his form of comforts; while the other sailors on watch navigated with the stars and Mayans charts. The other sailor kept his tabs on the boxes as the waves increased about his starboard north side of the vessel. The once steady lantern sways form side to side– in the direction of stern to bow, nautically east, then west. The crashing of the increasing weaves, jolts curiosity in the jackasses' erection. Then suddenly there was a Mayans dove descending from above the night's eye. Tied to its feet was a message from the elder chief. The noble sailor that manipulated the charts took gratitude of the inscription that descended with the dove.

Oblivious to the sailor's attentions, the moon descended in too. Unnoticed, the flared moon was distorted– but glowing with its delusional gleam; that was internally displacing molecules in all the worlds and villages' stream, rivers and seas.

Judging from the stars alignments on their location and what was in-scripted on the Mayans chart, the vessel was ascending into the deepest end of the open seas; 15 mile across the Bermudian triangle. Suddenly the dark matter of night fall has turned their nautical crossing into a blanket of pitch blackness… a sudden act of sailors blind– the stars were gone, there was not a trace of the flared moon… the squeaks of the lantern faded into mysterious mute— Dead, was the flames of the sailors light, but bright as the midday's light; was the jack-assess eye.

Notably, the waves that created many hours of sailors' motion and movements settled into the mute of delusion. This mood was eerie, dumb and deafening.

It was too quiet— for the sailors deceptions; even the asses' wanted to scream– but the two prize possession of the Mayans transportation; kept a gluten itinerary on the sailors' appetizers and home-made delicacies.

Intelligently, the sailors began to constrict the treasure-boxes securely to the wooden planks in the cargo area as instructed by the chief descended inscription. It appears the sailors were bracing for the foreseen events that was threatening the closing village.

The Mayans knew that a full distorted moon, created dynamic tides, which usually raises their suspicions. However, they knew it was a naturalistic event on their calendars. They also know the effects of such event on the open seas. Unfortunately, it was that particular time and event on the present charts and calendars. In addition it was etched into the sailors' inscription of Mayans foreseen notable knowledge.

There was something instilling and mysterious about the aura and mood on the Mayans reservation grounds as there was mystery on the sailor's seas.

The situation was deafeningly intense and motivationally quiet. The convulsing of the jackasses in the stables was over-powering. The activities in the wooden shacks grew tentative and silently weak. Something was upon the essences of the Mayans time.

The elder chief; calls upon a sudden ceremony, in the powers of astrology and the powers of his inscriber's intuitions and intuitive mind. Deep into the midnights light, the Mayans began another transcriptional foresight. They chanted the secrets codes and read the mysteries from the crystal skull as it was being depicted.

As time grew ever-more silent— dark and bleak; suddenly there was vibration and braying inside the asses stable. The elder chief, held a chosen dove gently as they sat around the table collecting the readings of this night's foresight. The inscriber charts a new course; to divert the sailor's vessel from disasters seen in the illumination of the crystal skull as the drifting of the currents pulled them into the Bermudian triangle.

He selects a special ink, as he continued to chart far their vessel from the foreseen disasters. He folds it neatly and he then gave it to the chief; who then placed it onto the obedient waiting dove. The chief whispers Mayans secrecy into the bird and open the wooden-window and watched as the messenger flared away in the open night.

Relentlessly, the messenger flew across the rivers for hours; it traveled across the open seas, in the eye of the darkness and passive aggressive breezes.

When the messenger had descended into the safety of the sailor's vessel, it settled upon the asses grass. Immediately after securing the boxes and sails, the moon resurrected its boastful flare. The ocean began to dance unsteadily, creating large swells as well as intrusive waves.

Instantly the condition went from suspense to dangerously rough. The three noble sailors joined their hands together; to call upon the powers of Mayans-good-lucks. They chanted the secret code, until the illumination glows bright from one of the boxes that was secure to the wooden planks. Momentarily, a large swell followed by a forceful rouge-wave threw the sailors vessel into the underside of the deep… the box of illuminated light rapidly sank below the reefs deep and like that it was all over and back to previous calms…

CHAPTER 5

The two young noble steeds, shivers with the sounding of their rattling teeth... not because they smelt the sailors food or feet– it was because their outer garments were soaked in the rapid seas; when the rouge-wave turned the vessel upside-under the reef's deep.

The sails of the sailors' boat, hung on a knotted rope; as the illumination descended further into the underworld of the abyss.

Many layers of the asses' straws, travels around in a floating drift— as the sailors eyes kept swift pursuit of the illuminated box that rapidly went into moonlight abyss... with a solidify thought imbedded in their mind that there was nothing they could have done to retrieve this box form the gravitational pull of the seas.

One sailor resets his sails in remand to maintain the objective: one cargo less as they honour to carry on the chief's duty.

For 30 days and 30 nights, the vessel drifts onwards from mid day, to mid night; mornings to sun sets, with a sailors lantern swaying east to west; two sailors on guard while the other consolidate his fair amount of rest– on the asses grass.

On the 27th day of the Mayans voyage journey; 3 days before they settled a shipper's anchor into the sands of the village shores, one of the noble sailor's whispers secrecy into the chiefs chosen dove and released it into the open surrounding-body-of-water and blue-backdrop.

The powers of its acting wings flopping; echoes across the blue shaded contrast of distance. The sound and its active flight disappears into the still of invisible distance in search of the destine village land.

For 3 days and 3 nights the obedient dove continued its directional flight with the sailor's vessel many nautical miles drifting behind on the open ocean. The horizon began to blend into the edge of the village's shore. 7 minutes later it descended onto the village sand and picks up a beak-full of sand-stones, sea-moss and evaded into the very direction in which it came.

A few hours later, the chiefs dove descended into the sailor's vessel with solid evidences of land that was in close proximity; across the nautical horizon.

The navigator that was on guard adjusted the sails in the direction that was coordinated by the descended dove.

Now it was only a matter of time and the drift of the winds before the sailors' would reach their avid destination.

But this morning when the sun placed light into their direction, they settled upon the village shores.

If the sailor's scope, chosen dove and Mayans charts had proven correctly, the vessel had settled upon this very location; 27,000 nautical miles from the Mayans reservation camp grounds, far-far-away!

One of the three noble sailors; exhorted a shipper's anchor into the village shallow, to secure the swaying vessel to a sudden still, then a shipper's stop!

He then steps onto the village shore to make a positive match of the sand-stones and sea-moss that the dove had carried back. He takes up a hand full of sea-moss and sand-stones and held it underneath the spectacle of his sailor's scope and made a positive identification with the sand-stones and sea-moss that was carried by the chief's obedient dove.

CHAPTER 6

The three noble sailors were relieved to have finally settled upon their destination after a month long journey. However, this amazing feat was short lived as they stepped down from the vessel– to stretch their mussels and regain the concepts of the mission on hand. With smile and Mayans pride depicted in their renewed demeanour, the memory of the illuminated box sinking into the darkest matters of reefs deep; had sunk in their minds nonetheless to say. Even though, they were one treasure box short of the mission, they had to continue as requested by the chief of their people.

One sailor presciently scratched his rear, followed by his head, in disbeliefs as well as joy outlined in his beliefs– that they had finally came to rest on the village shore; in doing so, he removed a handful of the jackasses hay that as acted as their comforting sheet and pillows. One sailor carried a shipper's rope beyond the village shore and tied it around the trunk of a solid mahogany tree; that stood embracing the sun; to prevent their vessel from relaying the messages of the currents, as the other sailor inscribed Mayan symbols onto the Mayans chart with his unique ink and feathers. He draws the surrounding into the chart of Mayans foreseen past and future, he scribbles secrecy in between the **golden** pigments. The simplicity of the time was just right!

Each wave that broke at the shores before hitting the vessel was calm– but it was strange to be so far-far-away from the safety of their reservation-camp-grounds.

Neurologically, the Mayans were much more than foreseers, believers and dreamers. They cared just a bit more about the lands, the air as well as all connected seas. They occupied and lived by the 5 elements of physics. They were a distinctive set of guarded people; pruned to travel beyond the foreseen and the acres of this world.

It was told for generation that the Mayans had many magical potion and they were intuitive to nature and astrology. It was also believed that they were the guardian of this world, overseers to say!

In a great aspect of it all, they were cursed, ridiculed, mocked, categorized and feared by communities and colonies of people beside their own. Some would say they were the freaks of witch-craft and black-magic as well. They could not deter their generation from the title of; devil-worshipers and evil-doers.

Within moments of arriving onto the village shore, the three noble sailors had accepted the challenges; thus accepting land and tranquility, to call the village shore and surroundings their home for the time being.

There was a magnitude of work and organization compiling on the long list of things to be done; before the night places its poor visibility upon the sailor's anchored vessel and secluded surrounding.

3 day ago when the sailor had whispered secrecy into the chosen dove, the message was that; the dove was to find a secluded remote part of the village, which is uninhabited by any members of the people and that was exactly what was granted onto their requests.

54 miles across the eastern front of the village, another cloud filled afternoon unwinds into the falling of the sunset... as the mist of mount-7 settles into the hearts of the villagers; it slowly settled visibly upon the-noble-sailors, on the other side of the deserted village land and surrounding shores.

As the mist traveled closer to the sailor's vessel, it carries secrecy and messages of the catastrophic event that had brought 3 of the wisest and most dedicated Mayans in this very location.

Suddenly a mass of darkness settled upon the sailors' thoughts. Sounds of discomfort could be heard coming from where the two young steeds rested on the compacted straws, as this drift of mist came avidly closer and closer.

Whatever it was; it was mysteriously understood by the sailors; they immediately released the chosen dove into the mist of mount-7– it ascended into the messages of the mist; slowly but gradually the chosen dove eluded all visions and suddenly it was sunlight as it was before.

By now; the three noble sailors had accommodated for some of the things on the to do list but they paused their doings to watch as this mysterious mist retreated back to the top of the mountain from which it came; taking the chosen dove that had vanished with it. One sailor accesses the asses grass, their water and food supply; to determine how much remaining hours they would have to sketch, inscribed, acetate and prepare before they set off through the jungle, to honour the chiefs duty and wishes.

The fish stock was deficient beyond low! Water was moderate however. But hard-dough-bread was in abundance; so was the Mayans liquor and lemonade.

In addition, plenty of the jackasses hay was stocked-piled in one corner of the sailor's vessel.

In the moment of reassessing their levels of food consumption, it was boldly apparent the empty space that once housed the illuminated box; stood silent but more dominant than the other spaces where all the chief prescribed treasure were kept; inside the cargo bay.

What were the sailors to do without the most valuable treasure of them all?

They knew it was impossible to return to the reservation-ground with such news; that they had lost the crystal illumination that held the powers of **life** and **resurrect**.

The three sailors knew there wasn't a replacement and they would rather-less be seen as unfit in the presence of the elder-chief and the rest of their people.

More so, there were only a handful of illuminated crystal skulls and each individual skull was placed in its destined location. Nonetheless, it could not be retrieved from the great depths of the ocean floor.

The sailors conspired upon many solutions but they could not coordinate one that was significant enough to retrieve the lost treasure of illumination. They wondered if it being a few nautical miles off its destine location would alter the actuation of its intangibility, its actions or purpose. Therefore, they decided to simply leave it in the belly of the seas.

It was impounded by the guard of the water gods, thus secured there; far out of hands and arms reach. ***It could not be tampered with before its call to duty!***

At the crack of dawn, they would gather the cargo from the galleys and set off to find the head villager and deliver the prospects of the chief's prescriptions.

CHAPTER 7

7,398 kilometres from the bottom of mount-7– at this very location, a spooky but humble man inscribes foreseen events into the pages of present and future history.

He does so in the darkest matter of each night...

Whatever he has inscribed into his calendars and picture-grams; mimics the very same reflections of the Mayans foresights and inscriptions. He inscribes the unknown by the eye of his ever burning candle, in his concave, faraway in his secret temple. His surroundings is filled with: ink, bundles of papers, feathers, candles and jars of magical potion and a large bowl of spiritual water; in which he sees the unfolding reflection of each foreseen event.

In addition to his collage of artefacts of foresight; in one corner of his hideaway, he stores many cans of: sardines, fruits and countless lofts of hard-dough-bread.

Just before he sets off on his journey of foresights; he drinks of the magical potion a concoction of: lemon, lime, vinegar, salt, rain-water, liquor-preservatives and medicinal herbs that packs a strong punch. He needs this concoction to withstand the brutality of the events that he relives time and time again.

He stares in his burning candle without the slightest bit of movement— as he falls deep into his focus of foresight.

Whenever he has found the domain to his trance of transferring the night foresight; he gets up from around the table at which he has been sitting motionless– for more than an hour. undisturbed by the strong emotional connections of the foreseeing anomalies; he walks up to the large bowl of water and submerges himself below the surface and held firmly until he's reached the end of the night's episode of foreseeing.

He then raps himself in a white sheet; weeping then sulking horrendously for long period of times, often kneeling on the floor; calling on his advisor who stood above the terrace that shelters the universe. When he has finally cleansed his soul, he walks over to the table with a blank stack of paper and begins another inscription with his dark inks and feathers...

At a very early age in his life; Mr. Metropolis began inscribing on the families front porch, until the identity of his gifts out grew the spaces where he would hide to inscribe in the eye of his ever burning candle. However, his curious ambition led him into his own temple of: magic, inscriptions, illustrated dreams and his very own field of mortuary forensics. In addition, he could tell the tales of history form the signs of astrology; in his special bowl of dark water that descended from his advisor that stood above.

Poor young Nostradamus' mind thinkers away as he inscribes the greatest disasters of mankind over and over again. The agony of it all has taken their tolls on his mind and aging body!

One night, Nostradamus was resting soundly when he was suddenly awakened by a strange but conclusive dream; unlike none he's ever felt or seen before. When he woke up; he saw the foreseen event unravelling in the glows of the centered moon that stood guard outside his rectangular window. He began to sweat profusely in his cold room. The warmness he usually felt from his ever burning candle was nonchalantly not present. He was not afraid for himself but more so, felt the pains and punishments of those that were brutally displaced then buried upon the hoofed imprinted mountain-7. He immediately records the apocalyptic dismay»» in the dark, in a strange mood.

For seven consecutive days, Nostradamus held the pains of what he saw as well as the inquisitions of the event that was implanted into the calendars of history.

It was not a matter of when but the factor that stated it was destined and bound to happen.

Mr. Metropolis's concern continuously grew for these people who were caught in the raptures of the seas. He knew if he told of this; his cover of secrecy would be lifted and he could face the death penalty; for practicing the art of black-magic and witchcraft.

Nostradamus knew he was innocent of any accusations of witchcraft or black-magic. However, he was simply living by his gifts and the unspoken languages of astrology in addition, the messages of transcended dreams that he'd received.

He was stuck between a rock and a hard place; holding a deadly transcript of foresight on one of his many scrolls; however, this inscription was callous– but there were prospects uncountable that astounded his visions from the *golden* reflections.

As time went by; the secrecy of his cover had been lifted and many of his dreams, visions and foreseen inscriptions had come to pass; leaving his army of doubters in deep consideration to his abilities of foresight. Somehow, they were unrelentingly callous about his prophesy; but now, they found themselves wanting his wisdoms and knowledge.

His foreseen knowledge of many destructions of life's vitality would not allow him to maintain selfishness!

He was a prophet; thus in charge of critical information; like those that conspired on the Mayan's reservation and the similarities between Nostradamus and the foreseers Maya people were written incredibly equally in their foreseen inscription.

Among his magical potion, there was a special concoction that his foreseen abilities had instructed him to obtain with imminent urgency.

From beyond a secret tunnel that led off into the hillside of a mountain, Nostradamus carried an old-milk jar, a hand full of salt and his age-old-lantern; up to the top of this solid mountain range, in search of the mist that channels into the early morning rain. In his small leather poach, Nostradamus had brought along his stacked papers, inks and feathers. He rested his milk-jar and lantern on top of a solid sand stone.

He opens his hand of salt as his token of offering and scatters it all around.

The dew like mist began to accumulate into the spaces of the milk-jar, until it was full. Nostradamus closed the jar and opened his heart of satisfaction.

A sudden down pour of anxiety rushed into his increased heart beat. Like the drop of a dime; Nostradamus intuitively began to immortalize the transcending descriptions into dialogue that could easily be read and indentified; as he congressionally inscribes the vision that took over his spirit and mind.

Mr. Metropolis held firmly to his stack of paters and his precise ink, in addition, his feathers. He draws a large mountain, on top of two men, he then **colours** underneath the **earth** with his **golden ink**. He placed a treasure like box beside the fishermen's nets and then sketched a shipper's anchor. He continued to sketch around the mountain, adding many fruit trees, crop-beds, farmer's tools and two young boy stood beside the treasure like box.

When Nostradamus was finished; he counted the hoofed imprints that he had also placed into the inscription; he stopped at the seventh and closed his ink container. But suddenly, he received additional information from deep within is trance of foresight; so he immediately unwinds the cover of the ink container; beside the treasure like box that was recently drawn, he inscribes the symbol of illumination that preserved **life** and **resurrect**; he then coloured the phrase {L3VI}.

Finally he had come to the end of his foresight— he slowly folded and placed the scroll and calligraphy pieces back into his small leather pouch.

In that rearguards; Nostradamus closed the milk-jar and retraced his steps back to his secret temple with his lantern as his guide.

When he returned to his table at the eye of his ever burning candle, he labelled the old milk-jar; The Chosen Dove and placed it beside the other concoctions of secrecy. On that note, Nostradamus decided to take his rest; he cuddled up underneath his knitted sheets, stretch forth is hand to put away the eye of his burning candle and guiding lantern, when his room was fully dark and coherent, Nostradamus went on to sleep.

CHAPTER 8

54 nautical miles from the heart of the village, the three noble sailors had grown impatiently still. Nonetheless, they were more than ready to deliver what they had brought from the month long journey; from far-far away!

During their time at the edge of the village shore, the three Mayan men had ample time to construct a large enough wooden cart; to carry the boxes and young asses into the heart of the village; thus, into the heart of each villager.

One sailor secured the boxes to the cart; with repeated knots on the shipper's rope; he then signalled the others that everything was accounted for. Therefore, it was time to depart upon civilization beyond the mist of mount-7.

For the first time in over a month, the three noble sailors were leaving the comfort and safety of the vessel, as well as the surroundings shores, which they had grown to appreciate.

Heroically; they ventured beyond the edge of the shore, into the thick vegetation forestry without a map; they would travel only by the foreseen inscription of the chief's visionaries and foreseers. In addition, the three sailors were following the secrecy of The Chosen dove that had ascended into the mist of mount-7 some days ago.

In contrary, this had been the last time the chief's bird had been seen. The three Mayan sailors followed a specific route into the village; with a bird's eye's view, from the birds IQ.

It was ironic to think of such daring adventure– as they continued on the path of the complete unknown. These men were men unlike others; they were pruned to honour. Thus; they were messengers of missions.

No one in the village knew of this forth-coming surprise, neither were the three Mayan men, boxes and furry jackasses had ever been granted a welcoming invitation!

Little did they know they were trespassers of the village-land!

Half way into the journey, the sailors had stopped to consolidate the remaining fried-fish, lemonade and hard-dough-bread that were left in the meagre food supply.

The two jackasses immediately improvised with the sailors' bites, by introducing hunger into their voices; with excitement filled yawns and wide open mouths at the smell of the friendly fishes that were fried.

One sailor insisted that they hid the fishes form the asses' scene, it merely caused a fight between the three. But I guess he forgot the size of: the nostrils on the two furry hoofing jackasses. They just could not understand why the two jackasses were so impulsive whenever they scented the sailor's food in the commuting breezes.

 As like the other entire feast that came and went; today's feast was just for the sailors. The young jackasses would have to settle with a hand full of Mayan hay...

Even though the two jackasses did not get to enjoy the hard-dough-bread, lemonade and fish-fry; they got 54 miles of jollies' ride form the sailor's divine elbow's grease. Let's just say they enjoyed the productivity that the friendly feast had delivered, in a locomotive kinetic sort of energy; from the three little Mayan men that always could!!!

The secret trail that the chosen dove had implanted into the three Mayan men; was 27 yards from the end of civilization of the village. as one sailor wrestled to maintain his grip on the handle of the cart; subliminally he was wondering if there was any chance the route could have led them on a course that less avoided the intensity of the bitter humidity that seemed to have led a head of their steps. He swats away all the traces of sweat that was downing into his vision.

With much persistence encompassing the power of the festive feast that they had consumed a short while ago, the Mayan men had reached the last 27 centimetres of this long journey; covered in the sweat of their brows. The strength of the accompanying sun had drawn all but 7 litres of water which remained a-linger in the reserve jar of water.

The three Mayan men rejuvenated their spirits for the very first time in over a month, when they heard the sounds of civilization that was descending on their location from all directions.

They wrestled to lift the cart above a viper's-tree that had fallen in the pathway.

54-miles later; one sailor etched the completion and beginnings onto the Mayans chart– because this was a moment of great accomplishments... but their story has just begun.

Suddenly a barrage of men and dogs circled around the three Mayan trespassers; holding their sharpened-protection-pieces in the retreat position.

The leader of the heavily armed men shouted out "who goes there— who goes there" he repeated over and again without a familiar reply.

The three Mayan men were astonished, frightened and remorseless; not to mention tongue-tied.

By this moment, the army of men had surrounded the three strange looking men.

The furious bloodhounds intensify the situation way beyond what the Mayans foresaw.

"Who goes there? State your declaration for the record or you risk immediate beheadings!" said the man in charge.

This was hard to imagine, not to mention witness. *"It was honourable,"* the three men had come in peace.

Suddenly the mist of mount-7 had captivated the mood; cascading a thick cloud between the Mayan men and the village army. The chosen dove had transformed into a white flag; that signalled the Mayan men were friendly intruders, not forces of foe.

One sailor opened the inscription scroll and handed it to the leader in charge; he pointed to the boxes and presented the cart generously.

The intensity of the situation had been defused but the problem was; a language barrier was separating the villagers from the three Mayan men.

The army of villagers took the three men to meet with the "elder-village-leader Sir: William, Levi the third."

The story of the three mysterious men and treasure boxes as well as the two furry jackasses had locally grown out of its covers, then spreading around the village like a wildfire spiralling out of control; causing curiosity in all corners, at each intersection as well as the neighbouring towns.

All the villagers then found themselves captivated by the story»» so they all took their time compiling onto the home of Sir William Levi the third; to catch a glimpse of the extraterrestrial event that had descended onto their village.

Some of the villagers shouted, "let us behead them immediately; once and for all"

As others protested saying, "show them leniency and mercies, benevolence in blessings for the travellers' generosity; they cried onto Sir William Levi."

While one group stated their livid opinion; shouting "mercy to the men of the bushes who has traveled from far." One large group had brought food for the men.

While others found insecurities in their disbeliefs.

Incoherently, a larger group had gathered among the crowd with their sharpened Amory, vocally they stated, "We will show them the easy way out of our village-land, let us at them!"

The story grew speculation and mockery out in the village street, it was adamant either sides of protestor needed a solution to resolve the faith of the three Mayan men.

However, the faith and judgement singularly rested on the shoulders of Sir Levi the third. He was stuck between the impossible of the journey the three sailors had concurred and defeated–then docking onto his village-shore.

With that amazement in his mind, Sir William Levi the third debated with much admiration and the dedication that it must have taken the three men; to generously complete this feat of travels; on the unsteady-circling seas, to rest on his village land with their token of gratitude treasures.

Finally, Sir William was ready to invoke his power and judgement on the faith of the three Mayan men.

He stood empowering the gathered crowd and spoke with his obedience; "silence you all... my fellow patrons of our land– I hereby grant the trespassers my at most regards of leniency and mercy– with high admiration for what they've accomplished and so should you all; with noble respects, they have traveled a great distance, so let us grant them a chance to tell of the mystery that they have brought to offer and share."

The silent villagers began displaying their regards with cheers and applauses.

A great sense of unity was felt as the divided sides became open to the solution of leniency for the Mayan men.

Suddenly the three trespassers became the heroes of the village-land and icons in the historic hearts of each villager.

While the three Mayan men gained high honours and the respects of each villager, they told of the catastrophic anomalies that were inscribed on the scroll that was given to Sir William the third.

They introduced the ideas of making iron form mineral, turning wheat into bread, herbs and spices form plants. In addition, they told of the importance of the transportation that could be provided by the two young jackasses; when they had grown a bit older.

For several days, the three men introduced many new ideas that would forever alter the way of life of each villager.

In that very addition, for several days sir William Levi the third found some of the things that the Mayan mad had introduce; fearful, lucrative, not to mention beyond his beliefs. He wondered if there was any truth to the ideas of astrological prophecies. He found the men to be too simple; to obtain such knowledge and foresights.

His train of thought was leading him to believe the men of the seas were delusional form overexposure to seasickness.

As Mr. Levi continued to put ongoing thoughts to the mysteries of the Mayan men, he wondered and worried that a month long ride on the unsteady seas must have made the Mayan men believed they were invincible and convincible to others.

He was overly sceptical... so he decides to return the favour of joke to the Mayan men– because he thought; the Mayan men were playing with his serious stature as leader of his village-land and his people.

Mr. Levi did not want the villagers to live in fear of the sun, the clouds, the moon or stars, so he would do what was best for his people. He was fearful his villagers would seek refuge in surrounding lands; this would spell disaster to his power and wealth. He gathers a few villagers of his army to coordinate his plans of attack on the noble sailors. His first objective was to return the three men back into the belly of the seas; before their ideas and fear of astrology had seeped into each villager; thus, leaving them vulnerable to seek changes and refuge elsewhere.

He told the gathered crew, to make enough bread with the recopies and wheat that the men had given as gifts. his instructions were to make as much to last the men a year and a half on the return journey, which would have taken them only a month and some days, give and take the conditional weather forecast.

His second undermined instruction was; to refill the sailor's fresh water supply with the national kettle; 100% over proofed rum. Refill their fried-fish supply and let us bid the three Mayan men goodbye at the edge of the village shore once and for all.

His instructions were coordinated as planned; swiftly and quickly!

Before you knew it; all the villagers had gathered at the edge of the shoreline; loading food supply and the three noble sailors back into the vessel; thus, into the seas from which they had came.

It was written in the sailor's logbook and Mayan charts that the objective of the mission went according to the chief's plans and wishes.

The swaying of the vessel drifted beyond the villager's cheers by the rapid emerging windy sails.

The three noble sailors assured each other that all was well; thus, preparing mentally for the month- long journey back across the seas. Therefore, anticipating the appreciation and credited respects of their guardian chief, as well as their home.

They were reluctant to be back in there reservation-campground, back into the lives of children, fellows and their wives.

Back in the village, Sir William Levi the third requested his army to meet him immediately. He then sent his men to disclose of the boxes at the bottom of a well that was no longer in use; rhetorically far beyond the reach of any of his fellow villagers prevision, sight or understandings.

When the men had returned, they drank rum and whisky and laugh hideously as they tossed saying this; "the three men of far, the burden, the potion and the joke is on you."

Late into the midnight, early into the approaching morning; the vessel drifted into the nautical winds, at a steady pace, while back at the village-land; Sir William Levi the third grins with his devilish sins.

The three noble sailors were Hungry and Sea ridden, so they exhaled their expressions by repeated yawning. The swaying of the seas had sent the hunger calling and the sailors were reluctant but they insisted on replenishing their needs.

Unannounced to the three noble men of Mayan decent this would be their last meal. The three gather around the food supply and began to pray, when the prayer was final, each man could be seen nodding his head. They passed around the fried-fish, fruits, fresh water supply and hard-dough-bread to consolidate on a friendly bite.

CHAPTER 9

1000 nautical miles from this very location– at which the sailors drifted upon the sometimes-unsteady seas; Nostradamus was once again awaken by a strange but conclusive dream– that forced him to cipher a new inscription; subtly as he'd seen the repeated dream in the still of the flaring full-moon when he was dream-conscious; thus, sober.

He hurried to his burning candle, with much burden hanging on his pride and shoulder; he sat around his table to inscribe the tales of this dream, with astounding accuracy and details. There was something puzzling him as he sat inscribing. He wept considerable. He was movingly touched by the scenes of this vivid vision that played repeatedly in his mind...

For 2-hours; Nostradamus wrote with his ink and feathers onto his stacked papers with admiration, affection and consoling emotions for the three noble sailors as he saw it in the moon and beyond his dream. It was apparent a catastrophic event was about to unfold beyond the glow of the moon; upon the sailors in the drifting vessel.

Before Nostradamus was through with this inscription, he fell from his chair as if something was terribly wrong. He was not imminently conscious, however, motionless convulsing on the floor. But his ever burning candle kept a warming eye at his location...

1000 nautical miles from that very location; the chief of the Mayans reservation-campgrounds was suddenly summoned to an immediate ceremonial inscription by his foreseers, visionaries and dreamers.

When he stepped into the room; he felt disparity, clarity and the dawn of destiny in the mood.   There was a dark matter in the aura, which lingers as if a reflection was casted in the still–– of a mirror.

One of his foreseers handed him a new scroll with the tales of the foreseen inscription.   He would sit at the table in full-out disparity; lost between each written symbols.   On this inscription, his foreseers, visionaries' and dreamers; saw that there was entity as their own, far away»» some distance in the eastern direction that they did not detected before or knew of his existence.

Nonetheless, the story was; he was sickly, motionless, slowly succumbing to his demise on his wooden floor.

As the concerns of the chief continued to grow, he understood the identity of this powerful entity; he came across the hieroglyphics' that translated: Nostradamus, master of foresight and prophecies'.   The chief immediately gathers 3 of his finest sailors, healers and philanthropists yet again; to journey the distance to try and save the individual named Nostradamus.

1000 nautical miles east of the Mayan reservation-camp-grounds, Nostradamus had falling into a deep trance when he hit the floor; he was motionless— but his spirit of foresights had traveled to a place far beyond his own dilemmas; where he saw the coming of the very end. He came across the Mayan-reservation-campground... however; it was deserted, unrecognizable and swallowed up by the moving earth.

Then suddenly there was movement, which came from the floor and sound of concessional cough grew out the door.   Nostradamus pulled himself up to his table and the presence of his burning candle.   He staggered his steps to his cupboard of concoction and picked up the jar that he had labelled: The Chosen Dove.

He made a new inscription faster than any he'd written before; to warn of the events that were vastly approaching the Mayans-reservation-grounds.

He folded it twice; he opens the jar of mountain-collected mist and spoke secretly until a white dove appeared on the rim of the jar. Nostradamus pointed in the western direction and tied his urgent inscription to his chosen dove and released it out his window.

Several days later; Nostradamus was found hunched over his window's ledge without a breath of life; but the eye of his burning candle shines brighter than ever before.

Before the three sailors had the opportunity to journey the seas to revive and heal the entity of the eastern location; there was utter devastation; the moving earth swallowed up the reservation-campground. All was lost!

5000 mile from the village shore, the three noble sailors had consolidated the food supply from Sir William Levi the third and fallen asleep; never to regain consciousness again.

The three Mayan men died of alcohols poison, which they had drunk plenty of thinking it was fresh water. The vessel drifted into the darkest abyss, never was to be seen by the eyes of humankind again.

CHAPTER 10

Many centuries had passed on over the slopes and valleys of the mountain range– but yet the mist and mysteries of mount seven presently remained in guard.

Countless families had exchanged chromosomes, DNA's as well as strands of traceable genes; therefore, following moving generations. The reciprocation of shifting generations had transpired many a times over and then commenced endlessly again.

Children had grown from boys, into men. Girls who once played in a wet pool had matured into women; who could produce offspring's as fruits and then returned into the earth's rule. The blemishes of the summer gardens stood presently on still– in a shaded cool; but out in the distance, a herd of feeding hoofs made the best meal in a patch of golden hay; as the afternoon falls into its nightly rules, the furry hoofers echoes the valleys with their violent brays.

Sound of thunders had sounded form above; the magic of the clouds colliding had created an electrifying fire show, each time this had occurred; it caused the showers to fall then washed the tides into the village's bay.

The movement of the fishing vessels swaying back and forth suggested the powers of the unseen; intrudes the peacefulness of the sand piles that circles the shorelines– then sets asunder into the hands of the avid sails.

The cries of the three noble sailors are validly imprinted each time the end of the circling seas reaches the villages oar; with concerns of the golden Childs birth.

But the only voice that soured above the village at this particular time was that painful screams and conformation of Edith...

...Excruciatingly unbearable, Edith could not maintain this agony much longer. All the pains Edith felt transpired into cries of telling agony, which eventually escaped the hinges of her windows» then into the abyss of those who had set and sent the inscription.

"On the count of three– push as hard as you possibly can" said the mid-wife that was in charge of delivering the baby that was inside of Edith. "You're almost through young love; just a few big pushes and you can consider yourself a lucky mother."

"Ready, one...two...three..." Edith began to push with all the energy she had left inside... it's been more than 7 hours» since she's been trying to deliver: *new life of the chosen* into the history of the village. "Push–push... you must maintain stamina with each of your breaths." Maebel was relentless with her method of inspiration; until a tiny body was fully out of its mother's womb.

From that moment on; *destiny* would surround its arm of protection in the *region of the chosen and the inscription insisted the earth would give prospects untold to its chosen.*

At approximately 7:21 pm that night; Edith gave birth to a baby boy, naming: Mustave Melvin-Junior Levi.

Tears of joy as well as tears of loss encompassing- hidden-sadness pours out from the deepest confinements of where Edith kept her buried secrets, as she tenderly consoles Mustave in her arms; she looks onwards into the future of new baby boy Mustave, hoping that his further was that of a king; solemnly embodying the elements as *gold.*

Edith was tremendously emotional and overwhelmed, in addition, ardently happy that her hours of labour were finally over and done with. "What a mess of an experience she utters silently to herself!" Glowing with deliveries reliefs, her emotions has brought her back into the arms of love and comforts where she one felt that reassuring presences. However, it was all transparency to our minds and eyes.

With that said; Edith's labour of love has just begun.

Finally, there was a new sense of inspiration. Someone has come just in time to heal old-wounds, thus; start new memories where old-tales were burning ominously bright. Mr. Levi had pledge his full and honest commitment as a motto of appreciation to Edith, as well as tiny little Mustave, the day he entered the history of the village. In addition, Mustave was a ***mirroring reflection*** of his very own.

Everyone's telling observation was that Mr. Levi, was overwhelmingly gratified with his grandson's additional embodiments to his family; because it was proudly plastered on his impressions and boasting demeanour.

Mustave, had begun outgrowing his tiny blankets, his favourite toys and attires. Constantly retiring old memories where new ones had taken up new emotions and mental spaces; in the lives and minds of Mr. Levi and his mother Edith. He grew vibrantly with tons of energy and a large appetite for his mother's homemade delicacies; such as: fried-fish, baked pudding, ripe banana, sweet mango, lemonade and last but not the least; hard-dough-bread.

Mustave was adorably handsome. He nurtured from new born to toddler; with the changing of his days which leapt to many months. He then grew up to count his many blessings, which eventually matured Mustave well beyond his baby years.

But while Mustave kept on growing, Edith and Mr. Levi had stop in the tracks of emotional growth; they were stuck between coping with adverse reality and finding the cause, yet searching for his peace and their closure.

Evidently, time wasn't a measure that waited on a single man, let alone a woman or child. Simply, life in the village became memories of other memories as time came then went.

The villagers knew it as; night and days, week to months; then eventually summed up another year at the ending of prolonged years.

CHAPTER 11

As a transcendent of his beloved forefathers, Mr. Levi the seventh grew up with his unfair share of the shameful legacy of Sir William Levi the third– but he was nothing like his ancestor; he was pure, conscious and hardworking. Nonetheless, he carried an enormous shame and burdens of that infamous joke his great-great-great- grandfather, played upon the three Mayan men; who had brought positive changes with beneficial messages to the village many centuries ago. The sad part was; no one had the opportunity to put the theories of the Mayan inscribed philosophies to trial because Sir William Levi the seventh kept their messages silently secret in the still of the underworld.

As to this very date; many still questioned the myth of the inscriptions as well as the tales of astrological anomalies that were encrypted. Comfort had grown over fears. As for many centuries; the villagers lived with astrological-apparition-shadows casted over daily sneers.

The fear of the myth grew ultimately into each villager, centuries up on centuries that it may have been; the three Mayan men were infinitely delusional about the inscription that was left in the past. In that very addition, what were the purposes of the many gifts that were granted to the village that very day, on which the three noble sailors had descended upon the strangers shores?

The act of Mayans kindness and sir William Levi's harshness had long since been discarded beyond the abyss; thus, un-faded from the mountain mist– but the memories of the three Mayan men washes ashore on a wavy-daily-constant-basis; with gentle whispers of their voices evoking the surrounding village. However, in spite of Sir William devised plans of closing every door on the Mayans truth; would one day surface form its buried roots!

Edith was fully responsible with her role and title as mother and caregiver of sonny-boy Mustave. As a result; she dedicated her full commitment to his present and future wellbeing. In that addition, Mr. Levi has equally committed his resources as well as his labour of love to Mustave's overall welfare and well beings.

Furthermore, in his personal affairs, away from his adorable little munchkin Mustave, Mr. Levi relentlessly battled with his fears. He also wrestled subconsciously to overcome the wave-demon of his recent past.

Many years had passed on by; since the gruesome-tide deployed and departed before destroying countless lives that were close to his heart... but he relives the terrible anomalies each time he was restlessly asleep.

Some nights, Mr. Levi would remember sound ideas from his dreams. Other nights, his fears were evoked by nightmares. He remembers clearly the instructions he got one fearful night– he was retired in the discomfort of sleep; a friendly apparition told him that ***prospects and peace was under the mist of mount-7.***

For many night and months on end, this friendly apparition kept directing Mr. Levi to the grounds of mount 7.

Mr. Levi was a true fisherman at heart, but he was suddenly humbled; thus, became fearful of the circling seas where he had once founded his platter of showmanship's and comforts; not to mention the title of best fisherman in the village.

Above the force-pull currents and uneasy waves, Mr. Levi respectfully gave his all to earn his season's quota, which usually stood dominantly over his competition.

In a personal confrontational dilemma, he needed to choose between love, fear and peace; in addition, his future, the present or a painful past.

Sometime not too long after he'd been instructed by his friendly apparition yet again, he decided to take a mind clearing walk— to the-out-skirts of the village, where his forefathers had occupied countless acres of desolate lands.

He chose to do so because there was a connection that kept surfacing in his dreams. Driven by his friendly apparition and paranormal scepticisms, he took to the bushes with bravery in his heart, memories in his mind and the absolute unknown expectation riding above his shoulders.

Needless to say, he kept a promise that he was destine to fulfill. His promises were: to be all that he could; in providing for Mustave, Edith and Kyro.

Mr. Levi kept his promises up right in the palm of his hands and surfaced in the vessels of his heart.

With each step taken on this venture to the village out-skirts, he wondered if and when there would be a promise of closure, which he desperately seeks.

The exaltation of his breaths– pushed him close and closer to his desolate lands; in the out-skirt's of the village.

When he finally arrived at his destination, it seemed as if the burdens of his forefather Mr. Levi the third had arrived there with him too. There was nothing fulfilling about the-bush-lands-of-the-out-skirt; nothing that would regulate or erect prospect of peace and or closure. So, he did what any man with deception would do; Mr. Levi sat under the biggest shaded tree and started to reflect on his life's memories, growing realities and beyond. It was obvious and justified, that it was time to pick up the pieces, to move in the forward direction; away from his nightmares and fears; faraway from a distressing past-revelation that he had. In addition, moving forward was the only solution to manifest the promises he made.

And there sat Mr. Levi underneath the tree... Consumed by his ongoing thoughts, memories and pain... he breathes in and out to capture a sense of purity...

"What is there in this place for gain– he asked the surrounding plains?" Instantly there was the sound of the wind at his replies, followed by a deafening pause of silence. Yet, an ongoing strain of guilt was measurable more deafening in his mind. He felt he was ultimately the only one to be blamed. He willingly owned the responsibilities for what had happened. "This is entirely my fault" he said. "And no matter what and how hard I tried, I could not in a million years separate the guilt that saddled these shoulders of mine."

Then suddenly a humble emotional Mr. Levi began weeping... while he continued to scrutinize the depths of all his empathy and sympathy. Sorrows brought his sadness out like a rushing wave he once felt, when he journeyed the seas of the surrounding village. Mr. Levi could be seen nodding his head repeatedly "no... no...no..." The sound of his cries uttered with weeping-full emotions.

"I never had the opportunity to say goodbye... Melvin he cried, Melvin my stallion Melvin, I hope you and Joshua remains shipmates forever."

The additional thoughts of Joshua brought his feelings forth in the form of additional sorrowful weeping and heaving cries. He was expressing his emotions that he had Longley suppressed.

His emotional breakdown was disturbed by a moving silhouette-apparition that captured his interests just off in the surrounding patch of trees. "I swear I just saw Melvin" he said out loud. "Melvin he called out, is that you Melvin?" But there was no reply. Unsatisfied by the disturbing silhouette/apparition, he decided to venture further into the woods, to identify if it was just his mind playing tricks with his vision... so, he sets off daringly immediate.

Needless to say, the silhouette/apparition from his vision was gone, just as fast as it had appeared but there was more than a dozen gathered stone, which had captured his ongoing interests. The pile of stone seemed as though someone had left them there in a compelling formation; one on top of another. "It wouldn't be strange to find shrines like these out in the-out-skirts; he thought to himself."

It was foretold that centuries ago; many surrounding lands were used as ancient burial grounds.

Emotionally drained and disappointed that Melvin was not what he thought he saw, Mr. Levi sat down on top of the gathered stones, when he sat down disappointedly hard; the force of him hitting the stone dislocated the pile. He then noticed that there was a lid underneath the stones as if something was being secretly concealed.

On that accidental account, Mr. Levi's interest's level rose. He then began discarding the bundle of stones to gain full access. When he was done, he found that there was a shallow well below the surface. "Just a hole in the ground, go figure" said Mr. Levi sarcastically. "What are the odds; I was led here to my resting place? Is this empty grave a sing? I already feel ghostly as is." Mr. Levi seemingly went with the flow. He stepped into the shallow like grave and lost his balance, it was much deeper than he had originally assumed. He was overly taken, therefore, startled by the depth of his fall. However, for the most part; he was okay, fully alive and still kicking; a few traces of shrubs and earth-particles that showed evidence of his fall. The small accident jolted his egos and woke him up from the sarcastic place in which he was mentally trapped.

What he thought was a gravely resting place, was a prison that **held the given gifts of the three noble sailors**. Little did he know there were connections between what he'd discovered and his forefathers; in addition, anomalies of the village! Mr. Levi could not comprehend or believe what he had stumbled upon– nor did he have a clue what was **unearthed**. It all seemed ancient like, crates, seeds and wooden boxes, jars and strange things never yet seen before. However, he was awe-struck with the scroll that was among the unique artefacts.

In the event of what he has discovered; it seemed as if the mist of mount seven had desired interests on his discoveries– because his surrounding was suddenly swallowed up by the cloudy mist that stood guard at mount-7. Visibility got poorer as the time of the hour hand circles itself over and again. The surrounding articles and artefacts which lay underground had vanished behind the mist.

CHAPTER 12

Hours had gone by since Mr. Levi had stumbled up on his treasure filled hole in the earth. He was exceptionally at the mercies of his find– yet positive that this discovery was to be kept as his secret and his secret only. With a large amount of gracefulness, care and precision not to mention curiosity; he made his way through each nook and cranny of each box, containers and jars before he stumbled on a scroll with ancient like symbols. A form of language he did not understand nor had he seen before. These unidentified symbols were meticulously drawn into place. Intriguingly enough Mr. Levi could depict the shape of a mountain and underneath the mountain had a *golden* color to its clarity!

Drowning with curiosity; he decided to take this ancient portfolio home, to study the characters that were in-scripted.

When he was through investigating the facts of all matters on hand, he replaced the lid in the very same location at which it was found and he then replaced the stones as if they'd never been touched– and made his way home with the scroll tucked neatly under his arms. In addition, he kept the nature of his discoveries in his heart; where he knew it would be safely hidden.

When Mr. Levi got home, he made a secret hiding place for his ancient scroll and laid his thoughts out on an open table; along with few seed which he had inside his pocket that came from inside the hole in the ground. There he sat once more, with more added to his think table. He pondered for hours on end, from sundown to sunrise and there it was; the *objective* written in his mental picture.

It seemed as if the sight of the seeds on the table had struck a growing idea. Somehow, a new idea has come forth from the apparition from his dreams, things in the hole he'd discovered and the plains of mount-7. "This may just be a positive revelation, a meaningful way for both setting my mind free of pains, in consequence provide for my family" he uttered modestly to himself.

"Farming" he blurted out loud, "time consuming yet authentically rewarding, almost a dry form of fishing" he added with his charismas. A thoughtful moment has suddenly transpired hope; as a meaningful smile grew proudly on the face of Mr. Levi. Whatever was the cause of him venturing into the-bushy-out-skirts-desolated-land, held the conclusions to a promising future and more! Therefore, form ancient discoveries would bring forth growth; from the idea that kept brewing in his mind.

CHAPTER 13

Life in the village became modestly modernised from the ancient ways of getting by. People had no obligations; they had to adapt the principles and ideas of ongoing changes for present and future generation. The tales of the past were kept not too far from the jackass' grass. Moreover, it has not leapt out of the hearts of those who knew the folklores of their ancestors.

Motor cars, trucks and motor bikes; overtook the karts and chariots of old times, which once occupied the village's streets... but the presence of many jackasses were just across the pastures and fields, ready to carry disconcerting loads in its hamper whenever need be. A stubborn jackass would always alleviate the weak.

The mist of mount-7 stood guard at the top of the mountain... in cometh the ever moving waves, and then its momentum broke at the village's shores.

Numerous resorts had occupied the village's best beach-fronts. Foot prints of so many are visible in the golden sands. Before you knew it, our little village was transpiring into a Desirable boom town; filled with peoples from all corners of the globe and all walks of life; they came flocking into the village, to enjoy its beauty and peace of mind; cheap land and all that this unique place had to offer.

The mayor of the village along with members of his congressional party; has constricted a daring plan to get the village developed faster than it was already being constructed. Their plan would bring in additional funds;

to build roads, resorts, schools and a better hospital. In addition, such ambitious endeavours; if it was successfully promoted to the people of the village and visitors from abroad,

Would allow more jobs; as well as stabilize an international platform, so that the village would be at the top of all destinations; for those who wanted the most exotic yet comforted filled experiences.

Not too long after the ideas were conceived; the mayor held a public meeting with the villagers. His words of encouragements resonated throughout the loud speakers, then into the thoughts of each villager. Respectably, a few visitors took his inspiring speech into their considerations. They thought this was a brilliant idea indeed;

Therefore, they were ready to buy into the idea themselves.

Mr. Mayor was keen on the delivery of his promotional inspiring speech. His words and method of delivery were chosen very carefully. more or less, the objective of his criteria's was that: his government was prepared and upright willing to sell surrounding lands to anyone who was interested in a piece of the booming village.

Prices were sought to be dirt-cheap. Within a few months of him delivering his promotional pitch, thousands of acres of the village-land were already bought, surveyed and sold.

Mr. and Mrs. Dubwise were among the villagers who stood embracing the message of the village mayor. They were almost at the retirement stages in their careers, with that said; it was only a matter of time before they would openly buy into the village's land, sea and air.

Among the neighbouring list of villagers; there stood Mr. Levi, Edith and Mustave as well. The occasion was for everyone to understand that this could potentially be an investment opportunity of a life time. For those who could see beyond Mr. Mayor's speech; would distinguish that a piece of the booming village— a few years down the road would worth substantially more, than what it was worth at the time of purchase!

Those who were in possessions of monies, bought into the village what they could afford and those who didn't have substantial cash, gave a deposit along with a promissory note, that stated; they would continue to pay the remaining monies on a monthly basis, until it was no longer an outstanding account.

The surrounding lands were respectfully sold on a first to arrive first choice in location basis. If you had the cash, you pick the spot, and then consider it yours.

On that note, every buyer wanted the most exotic locations, closest to river-fronts, beach-front and close enough to roadways; so it was attainable in its access. Unfortunately, for those who waited these exotic locations were sold out!

However, all but few had not yet claimed a piece of their own village land.

CHAPTER 14

Even though Mr. Levi and Edith continued onwards with their given responsibilities in life, there was always that lingering emptiness, a shadow that followed their every movement. On the other hand, little Mustave was a replica of that very shadow's reflection, which at times made the journey of life exceptionally easier for both Mr. Levi and Edith.

The nature of their emptiness had settled into their souls– but mentally and physically this dark shadow was constantly taking its tools... but whenever you saw Edith or Mr. Levi, they were always represented by a brave face; yet that lingering question of the very shadow that was once a part of their all»» was also imprinted.

Mr. Levi had been thinking long and hard about the nature of his promises and the circumstances of the future, which include Edith, Mustave and the shadow of his emptiness... as he tried to make sensible justifications of his reoccurring nightmares as well as his ongoing dreams. Mr. Levi had not once implemented a thought for himself. Needless to say, he was all about his family and making the most of any decision that would be the results of his judgments. {Family first was his motto.} While he continued to put theories and causes to his apparitional instructions and nightmares, he was relentless to walk away a victorious winner. He wondered if putting two solutions together into the form of an idea; would and could benefit the entire family. After he carefully assesses his ever present thoughts and ideas, Mr. Levi was ready and therefore willing to move forward and risk it all.

He'd finally had a plan— at the end of his dilemmas.

Convinced that his idea was worthy and utmost presentable, Mr. Levi went to the village mayor, to see if there were any possibilities he could purchase a piece of village land with his savings; before the village lands were all gone.

Two days prior, Mr. Levi gathered all his monies that were in his possessions and those that were in other institutions became pending funds that would be gathered also. He knew that this was a major commitment and it would take all his dedication as well as his aspirations to become a ***prosperous farmer***.

Nonetheless, he emptied all his bank accounts, insurance plans, life savings as well as monies he had around the house; to bring his idea to life. There was no room for failure; his reputation and monies were hanging in the balance.

Trusting that the friendly apparition from his drams would turn his sadness into fruition, Mr. Levi sat down to discuss the matter with the village mayor.

"Good morning Mr. Mayor, it's a beautiful day to do business" said Mr. Levi.

"most definitely" replied the mayor, " I am glad you've taken the initiatives and the time not only to consider this option– but I am glad you've decided to come on by today." "Well Mr. Mayor, as you already know— my fishing career was taken away unjustly, sadly and unexpectedly." Mr. mayor sensed the sadness in the tone of Mr. levis voice and gave him the moment to reflect and sombrely console his losses and put away any trace of the empty shadow that were present…

"As a true friend of the people, tell you what Mr. Levi…" said the mayor, "today is your luckiest day ever, he added with a meaning full amount of inspiration.

"We all remember that day of your lost— as if it never left our minds or breaths, how could we have forgotten? Ever since your devastation; amberjacks, sardines and crabs are hard to come by in our village. You were the only reasonable fisherman in the village. And I must say we miss that dearly, we understood the nature of your losses and I am prepared to do a small token of appreciation and justice as a courtesy of repayment to you losses. give me 70% of your monies that you've brought, keep 30% and consider that entire mountain -7 yours, I know you will find prospects, peace, prosperity and yourself– as well as all that you've been searching for at the misty terrenes of mount-7..."

Mr. Levi was presently in total disbeliefs— he was at a loss for words– but he mustered up and arguably expressed "Oh thank you Mr. Mayor, you are too kind. What will I do with an entire mountain Mr. Mayor?" asked Mr. Levi. "You do with it whatever you wish; but my advice would be: ***do positive work and your prospects will be at earths reap***. It is all yours" Mr. Mayor replied.

The mayor insisted he took the offer because he admired his positive ethics as a former fisherman of the village. More so, Mr. Levi was an asset to the people. There was nothing Mr. Levi could have done but handed the mayor the 70% as requested. Mr. Mayor was adamant he took mount-7 and appreciate his kind courtesy.

Mr. Levi was entrapped between a rock, a hard place, Mr. Mayor-himself and moun-7.

"Use the remaining monies to get you farmland situated; you will make an awesome farmer. I cannot wait to enjoy the fruits of you labour" said the mayor.

"And you will be the first, without any doubt to eat of my crops." replied Mr. Levi. "That is a promise" he added.

Mr. Levi was ecstatic to sign his land titles and deeds… when all was said and done; they shook hands and gave a tap on each other's shoulders. Mr. Levi was a happy man when he left the mayor's office. Overflowing with excitements, he could not wait to get home and share the news with Edith and Mustave.

When Mr. Levi finally made his entrance trough his house door, his positive conspiracies were felt. Edith began reflecting the positivisms which circled the room. "Have you gone fishing again dad, Is that why you seem so happy?" Mustave asked. "No son" replied Mr. Levi.

"What has put you in such a vibrant mood, may I inquire" asked Edith?

"The hands of karma have touched me with a mountain of blessings, worthy of my vibrant mood" said Mr. Levi. Little Mustave and Edith were curious to decode Mr. Levis term of hypothesis; but Mr. Levi would not let them wonder too long or hard; he was willing to share the joys of his good fortunes and news.

"You wouldn't believe how lucky I am feeling at this moment; a Good Samaritan has given me more than the quantity of hope I had planned to bargain for. The mayor of the people is definably a mayor of our people!" Mr. Levi explained.

"What on earth are you saying?" Edith asked.

"Let's just say; things are looking up respectfully and positively, it appears all hope had not been lost and our guardian angel has spoken on our behalf today. Come said Mr. Levi, follow me", Edith and Mustave approached the doorway behind Mr. Levi. "Look ahead—»» that entire mountain belongs to us." Both Edith and Mustave were quiet surprised. "What will we do with that entire huge mountain?" asked Mustave.

"Son, we will plant vegetables, fruits as well as seeds of love and seeds of secrecy" he explained with knowledge from beyond. "There are many questions you all have in considerations— but only time will answer them all." replied Mr. Levi.

The mocking of the village people

People in the surrounding village thought that Mr. Levi must have been out of his mind to buy the entire mountain-7.

"Ha, ha, ha, they laughed; what a clueless moronic man. It seems not only did he lose the Spaniard, his deckhands and his aspirations for fishing-amberjacks, crabs and sardines; it also seemed as though he'd lost his marbles, his mind and more.

I guess he could not afford a desirable-exotic location like the rest of us. Look at our oceanic-views and all you can see up the mountain are large eyesore-boulders, forestry and oh yeah, a cloud of mist that condensate the entire island. Expressively pathetic"

The idea; that Mr. Levi was undertaking such a colossal task as farming, resonated scepticisms and a higher conception of negativity around the village.

Some of his rival fishermen spoke "that his idea of farming mount-7 was lucrative; it was not that bright an idea, furthermore it wouldn't bring forth fruition; not up in the misty terrain of mount-7."

On the other hand, other lousy fishermen were simply overjoyed that he was finally away from their embarrassments. They said "it was to damp and cold an atmosphere, besides the oxygen levels was too low; for plants such as fruits and vegetables to grow." But little did they know, Mr. Levi was not a sceptic man, their negativity did not deter or distract him from trying.

One of his former competitions uttered; "maybe he is trying to get closer to god, which must be the ultimate reason why he bought the mountain-7." However, the funny news was that– Mr. Levi wanted to be as far away from the ocean-front as possible. Faraway form the haunting that held him captive and no progressive for so long.

His lucrative idea was however set in stones, set in mind, thus; it was set in place and written by the minds of ancient prophecies.

Driven by that hope and inspiration given by the Good Samaritan Mr. Mayor as well as the apparition from his dreams, Mr. Levi began the daunting task of removing the seeds and containers form his desolate hole in the ground. It took many trips to and from the-out-skirts of the village to remove the quantity he needed. However, Mr. Levi was driven by his willpowers; until the task was completed.

The idea was: to plant as much as he could at the lands of mount-7. Therefore, there will be bountiful rewards when it was time to reap of the harvests.

He knew this adventure would be time consuming and physically demanding– yet he was poised to make prospects, progress and prosperity on this idea as well as the promises he made. There were much to be done before the farmers season began and the negative monologue of the village people only added fuel to his fire, which intensifies his drive. There was so much preparation before he was ready to place the first seed in the ground... needless to say; there was nothing that stood between his determination and all the work that was to be done.

CHAPTER 15

Mr. and Mrs. Dubwise, had longingly been dreaming of building their retirement mansion in the village. After purchasing some acres of the village land, they've come to break ground on their dreams.

They hired the best construction company– to make good on their epic dreams.

This undertaking was to be one of the best homes in the noble village. Mrs. Dubwise instructed the foreman of the construction company; that in addition to building a massive mansion for the two, simultaneously they were also to build a stable big enough to house 2 dozen lucky stable-mates. As a retired veterinarian, she was modestly concerned for the animals she was planning to care for— but most importantly, she was eager to get them trained, to enter the annual jackass derby; which was a gambler biggest dream and sometimes became their biggest nightmare. In addition, the national jackass derby brought festivities, livelihood as well as the jolliest form of entertainment to the locals in the village.

Lead by firm instruction by Mr. and Mrs. Dubwise, the construction of the mansion and the stable was well on the way.

Mr. Dubwise had been searching to find a medical institution to lend his experiences and found the perfect place in the local hospital to practice from.

The construction company advised them that a project of such a magnitude could take anywhere from 8 months to a year; from foundation to full completion. However, as a precaution measure; they would work around the clock to have it done in 6 months. This was morbidly impressive information to the Dubwises'; they could not wait to settle into their mansion, to enjoy their retirement as well as the village.

6 months later, Mr. and Mrs. Dubwise received the key to their brand new house and stable. Slowly but surely they settled in— two weeks later Charlie and Jacob had moved into the spacious stable too

Life was perfect for the Dubwises,' they've been blessed with all that they'd asked for; sunshine, beaches, good food, a mansion and good neighbours. As each day turns to night, little Jackie and Jacob grew bigger with the care of Mrs. Dubwise and the help of ancient Mayan hay. Before you knew it the tow jackasses had reproduced which meant: there are more hoof and mouth to feed in the spacious stable.

Mrs. duwise was emphatic to have had four young cubs joining the family, she's spent the last year and a half training Jackie and Jacob to sprint like a stallion across the national jackass derby's finishing line. However, a word of advice was given to her by the wise; a stubborn jackass does what it feels; whenever and howsoever it feels Mrs. Dubwise. This was the main reason why the jackass derby was so entertaining– because them group of donkeys were stubbornly unpredictable.

Mrs. Dubwise had been dreaming of competing in the derby ever since she'd set foot on the island many years ago; and saw the festivities happening on by from the window of the tours bus. Nonetheless, she thought lesser of the advice she was given about the unpredictable behaviours of one to all jackass. The good news was; time kept on turning enough so that the national jackass derby was slowly approaching on the wheel of destiny.

Mrs. Dubwise wasn't as keen on becoming the best competitor among those who were set to compete, more so, she simply wanted to share and be part of the festivities that took over the village once a year.

It was more a competition for bragging rights or you won the laughing stock of the town– with you silly jackass, which seems to have been the repetitive outcome to every national jackass derby that has been kept centuries ago. There wasn't much of a reward for best runner; a modest trophy, a bale of hay and a sturdy length of nylon-rope. The positive news was that; it was all about the jackasses and that is how it will and should forever remain.

Days before the competition were set to commence, the stubborn furry hoofers gallop up and around the village with stability, ancient morals and unruliness outlined in their behaviours. Traces of jackass hoofs are left behind in a pile of its own shit. A group of unruly jackass ran in the opposite direction, from which its owner had instructed it to converse, it was historical to the children who watched from the opposite side of a church. The entire village was preparing for this year's annual derby, except for the competing jackasses themselves.

On the day of the much anticipating event, the mist of mount-7 circled the island and captivated the village for hours on end; until moments before the derby began, the mist then suddenly dissolved into the stands. The condensation build up around the village had cleared.

There was a spiritual feel as though there was a presence among the livelihood of the national jackass derby— it was puzzling, troublesome and it was unexplainable.

Was there more beyond what the eyes could see?

It was spoken of by our ancestors: that something paranormal was causing and controlling the racers of the derby; manipulating them into doing unpredictable things from which they had been trained to do. How was it that the jackasses forgot their lessons of stride and stability and ran off the track— in the opposite direction?

Every villagers has vowed is or her experiences of feeling something abnormal at the event whenever it was kept. Traces of the national-brewed-liquor along with a disobeying-pungent-smell that come from men that had been at sea for months; over powers the benches at the derby— but the stench of sardines was one that remained in the thoughts of each villager who attended the derby.

It was a beautiful day to sit and enjoy another jackass derby. At last, Mrs. Dubwises' opportunity of entering the competition was only moments away from bridging the gap between dreams to reality. She could hardly contain her excitements— as she made a few last minute adjustments; to her team mates Jackie and Jacob. The entire village had descended onto the grounds of the local stadium; all the benches were full from top to bottom. Mr. Levi, Mustave and Edith have come to show their support to the furry hoofing racers. The mayor of the village was also present too— so was Mr. Dubwise. The entire locals were accounted for. Moments before the festivities were set to begin– a sudden up roar alleviated form the crowd; asking "who had brought the smelly sardines?" A group of individual on the opposite side describes "that something or someone stunk of the national-brewed-liquor and carried a seaman's pungency." "It sure inst me" replied a local drunk in the crowd. He was very much sober, so there was truth to his prophecies. Everyone began to chuckle.

But the sound of the national anthem brought the crowd back to their respectable attention.

The games were finally ready to begin! Everyone has waited a year for the outcome of today's national jackass derby.

Beyond the festivities and what each villager's eye could see, there was Mayan magic at hand. The three noble sailors had returned from the depth of the traveled ocean, each time the national anthem had been sun to start the jackass derby; they were always present to share in the festivities too.

Their presence could not be seen. However, it was detected by the stench of sardines, seaman's musk and the smell of brewed liquor.

It was fair to say: the three Mayan sailors have come in peace; in the form of spirit to provoke as well as tease the furry hoofers and give the villagers a solid dose of laughter at the entertainments complex.

The moment all had been anticipating has arrived; 7 of the furry racers have taken up position at the starting line, so did one of the Mayan sailors. He stood at the finish line with a bucket of sardine, in utter patients for the jackass to arrive. "This auth to be funny" said one sailor; who sat in the stands with his hands clutching his brewed liquor.

The crowd began to cheer— they were all eager to place their bets. The announcer began the countdown 1– 2– 3– And the gates swung open; the furry racers were off with strength and stability in all their strides, another sudden up roar came from the crowd... the jackass derby has finally begun.

Tails were flying, hoof were kicking and jackass teeth were widely grinning as they went down the tracks– but suddenly all the jackasses had come to a complete stop and went back in the direction from which the race was started... all that the spectators saw was a cloud of residual dust created by the brake pad of the furry jackasses. The up roar of the crowd went silent— and anonymously toneless. The two sailors in the stands were historically laughing at what has taken place. What the villagers failed to see; was that one sailor was tossing sardines in the opposite direction, which caused the jackasses to follow swift pursuit. Even though it's been many centuries since the sailors had brought the furry hoofers onto the island, they were still glutton for punishments. No one understood the jackasses like those of Mayan decent.

Every villager who placed a bet had lost his and her share, trainers and owners of the furry racers could not justify the behaviours of their racers. Jackie and Jacob were no exception to the sailors sardine mockery. The national jackass derby had not crowned a winner in this year's competition. The stench of the Mayan spirits has disappeared– and the village was back to normal. Nonetheless, the jackass derby was filled with its shares of entertainments. Even Mrs. Dubwise had her moment of shine.

When Mr. Levi, Mustave and Edith was set to disembark the stadium grounds, he receives a tap on the shoulders from Mrs. Dubwise; "good day to you all" she said. "Good afternoon" they replied. "Are you that individual who has been working up in the hills of mount-7" she asked Mr. Levi? "Well yes I am" Mr. Levi replied.

"I admire your dedications" said Mrs. Dubwise "and it's been on my conscience seeing a hard working man such as yourself– voyaging up and down the hills with such heavy loads as you carry and I thought you could use a young strong stable platform to help carry your loads." Mr. Levi was speechless— he had no idea that anyone was observant of his hard works and dedications, he could not find a sentence or phrase to reply. Mrs. Dubsise continued with a courteous jester, she said, "I have more than enough stallions in my stable that can do you a lot of justice, come on by to the house and chose one of my stable-mate. Bring the family, me and my husband will be waiting." "I do not know how to thank you" said Mr. Levi. "I am thankful of your courteousness and when all is ready of my crops I will return my appreciations. I will come by on Monday as you insisted, if that is okay with you?" "Most definitely, Monday is acceptable" said Mrs. Dubwise.   "See you then and thank you so much" said Mr. Levi.

"That is awesome dad" cried little Mustave, "you get to chose your own donkey! Maybe I could take him to school too... and teach it how to read and play marbles."

"I highly doubt you'll be able to teach a jackass to do anything because their capacity for learning is beyond miniscule" said Mr. Levi.   "I bet my donkey will be my best friend in the whole wild village; *I'll give it my lunch, breakfast and dinner.*"

"I bet you will son, I bet you will", said Mr. Levi.

"That is so nice of them to give you a young stable-mate to help you with the hard tasks at mount-7" said Edith "and the best part of this is: people are seeing your dedication and that is a reward a lazy sole will never encounter."

"I am so proud of you Mr. Levi and I know Melvin is too", she said with a sadder note in her speech.   Mr. Levi wrapped his arms around his family as they all shared in the courteousness and sadness that was felt.

CHAPTER 16

"If only there were other genuine Samaritans such as our mayor and Mr.& Mrs. Dubwise residing around this village, maybe then this place could be called paradise after all." said Mr. Levi as he walked up to the driveway to pick his stable-mate from the Dubwises' residence.

"This is quite a mansion" he utters sincerely before he rings the buzzer.

"Mr. and Mrs. Dubwsie, seems to be living very comfortable– yet they are a kind set of outsiders" he added to his monologue in thought.

"Good morning Mrs. Dubwise." "Well good day Mr. Levi– I am glad you've made it. Where is the rest of the family" she asked.

"Well... unfortunately little Mustave is off to school with the assistance of his mother Edith. Maybe one day soon; one of your stable-mates will be able to do more than just farm duties; maybe it will also take Mustave to school."

"Well"... said Mrs. Dubwise, "that is understandable and there isn't a load around this village one of my jackasses couldn't carry. My husband is off to the hospital too, so it is just you and I today."

"Well, come on in and make yourself at home... this way!" she said, "The stable is just off to your left."

"This is quite a place you have here Mrs. Dubwise!" said Mr. Levi. "Thank you!"

"It is quite lavish; however, it's all a reward of our hard works and years of our devotions to our careers. Needless to say Mr. Levi, this is where we humbly call home." replied Mrs. Dubwise. "Just a few more steps and we should be entering the stable."

Mr. Levi was amazed by the size of the stable, it was large enough to comfortably store a hundred or more of the furry hoofers– but to his surreal surprise; Jackie, Jacob and four young cubs were the only ones residing in the spacious stable.

Mrs. Dubwise opened the stable doors and they walked in... Jackie and Jacob ran to greet the pair with their jackass's excitement. Following behind, was four month old Konrad. He was an adorable little stallion, full of energy; big bright eyes and a jackass grin»» filled with oversized teethes.

"Well hello" said Mr. Levi... "Seem as if my choice isn't going to be that difficult." Little Konrad ran up to Mr. Levi and sat down.

"I think... I will take this one, if it is alright with you Mrs. Dubwise?" He mentions with admiration in his voice. "If that is your solemn choice, consider him yours Mr. Levi!" replied Mrs. Dubwise.

Mr. Levi and Konrad had struck a lasting connection from the very first time they met each other.

Mrs. Dubwise was emotional with the departure of Konrad; however, she knew that it was a good deed. Mr. Levi showed his appreciations to Mrs. Dubwise. He then took his furry jackass Konrad and went home.

While Mustave was at school, he told his classmates that soon; he will be taking his new transportation on its maiden voyage; a test ride so to speak, to see how efficient of an investment Konrad would prove to be.

"If he couldn't carry me to and from school, the jackass that rested in the yard at the roots of the massive mango tree, was worthless." he told the class and they all began to chuckle.

In addition to his conversation with his classmates', Mustave was adamantly spoken that his transportation would become another one of his best friend; to increase his best friend count to an impressive number that will indeed equal two; Konrad and Kyro.

At 11:45 am, the lunch bell interrupted the conversation. Mustave and all the other students, hurriedly went to the canteen; where he took pride in devouring his; 2sunriped mangos, 2 slices of puddings, 2 crispy well seasoned fried-fishes,4 slices of hard-dough- bread and a jar of sugar-doused-lemonade.

In addition to, Mustave found room for his two whole ripe bananas, before you knew it he was out cold... out for the count— on the canteen bench.

As usual, he was awoken by the end of day's bell. Before Mustave was satisfied that he made the best of the lunch his mother had prepared; he taps one the bottom of his lemonade jar... he held it up right to his head, to wash away the small residual remains of sugar, lemon-pulps and lemon-seeds.

After Mustave had cleansed his lemonade jar clean of any residual residues, he made his way home with a substantial amount of excitements and eagerness to meet his transportation with a sweet tooth.

At last, Mustave could see the end of his eagerness and excitements in sight, just a few more steps remained and Mustave was home. He could see Mr. Levi underneath the massive mango tree attending to the transportation with many admirations.

"Get over here" cried Mr. Levi. "Come and meet Konrad, isn't he adorable?"

Msutave ran to meet Konrad for the first time. "This is Konrad son."

"Hi Konrad" said Mustave. "Can I take him to school tomorrow dad?" Mustave asked. "Unfortunately son, he needs to develop the strengths and stability before he earns the title: jackass, the master of all bearing loads; before he is able to do any hard labour.

For now, you need to treat him with respects as well as fair sharing's, which means you are in charge of taking care of Konrad until he is able to help out." "No problem dad", Mustave replied with his sense of assured responsibility. "I will do all that is required of me."

From that day on little Mustave and little jackass Konrad began growing together and sharing in the spaces that contained the air they breathe. However, there was something indistinctive that separated the two.

Eventually that day was upon us, when Konrad had to make that transition form backyard pet, to the Levi's locomotive. Mr. Levi had given his patients in order for Konrad to growingly develop that mature jackass ability»» to carry **loads** and today that patients was replaced with a well made jackasses hamper.

In retrospect's, something was affecting the health of Mr. Levi, which was causing him to lessen his loads to and from the hills of mount-7. Therefore, Konrad would have to pick up maturity and then pick up the loads as they were needed to be moved to and from one location to the other.

It was also time for Konrad to make his grand entrance through the school-yards Iron-Gate with passenger Mustave aboard the maiden ride.

Early the following Monday morning, Mustave got up from his bed, the smell of fried-fish and fresh hard-dough-bread crisping away on the pot-of-hot-crackling-coals reminded him why he was able to crawl in and out of bed at nights and in the mornings. Edith was busy in the kitchen, preparing today's share for the family. Mr. Levi had already left to maintain the crop-beds at his farm-grounds on mount-7. However, before he departed, he'd left firm instructions that Mustave was to follow; please attend to Kornad-our-transportation, before he took you to school.

Mustave carried a bucket of water and a hand full of salt to Konrad, who was fast asleep underneath the massive mango tree. "Rise and shine sleeping beauty" said Mustave. "Here is your breakfast" as he violently slams the bucket on top of Konrads' hoofs; he rose quickly from his momentary sleep. Konrad was a bit cautious and startled by the wet awakening and a hand full of salt that flew into his ear.

After attending to his transportation, Mustave went back into the kitchen for breakfast.

After breakfast, Mustave was neatly attired in his uniform. Kornad has relocated himself from mango tree, to kitchen steps, where Edith was preparing lunch for share.

Kornad was pleased to count the items on today's lunch menu; 2-mangos, 2-banannas, 4-slices of hard-Dough-bread, 2-slices of freshly baked pudding, 2-crispy fried-fishes well seasoned for taste and a jar of sugar filled lemonade.

Konrad was not insecure about his fair shares because he was overly certain to attain half of the portion at lunch.

He was full of energy to take Mustave through the village to school for the very first time.

Edith gave Mustave her affections, his lunchbox and a few kind words of advice as well as encouragements before he went through the door.

"Do not forget to share the lunch portions equally between yourself and Konrad. Be good and pay many attentions to your teachers" said Edith.

Korad's two gigantic satellite-dish-like-ears, discreetly eve's dropped directly into the conversation, he was sure that conformation Edith gave Mustave about the order in which the lunch was to be equally divided; there would be no mistaking it when the lunch bell sounded at around noon later today. Mustave replied "yes mother." He then carefully with excitements led his transportation out of the yard and straddled himself into the jackasses hamper, to enjoy his maiden voyage through the village, to disembark exactly at the school yards Iron-Gate.

Halfway on the journey to school, Konrad was no longer excited about this endeavour; it seemed that the hand full of salt from breakfast has caused him hunger and thirst. Konrad was itching for a feast to bite. In addition, the smell the came from the lunchbox added a substantial degree of taunting and discomforts to his every steps.

Konrad tried to maintain his innocence's of hunger— but the salt he ate earlier has gotten the best of him. Konrad kicked Mustave away from the safety of his hamper and ran to find a patch of hay and drank gallons form a stream that was nearby.

Mustave's attire were rumpled and filled with jackass-fur, when he finally made it to Scholl. Mustave tied Konrad at the Iron-Gate on the school property and went on into his classroom with his share of the embarrassments.

Mustave hid his bruised ego inside his lunchbox– where it was fortunately not visible and vowed to repay his dividends to Konrad, who was waiting by the iron-gate.

Mustave was however still proud to show off his disobedient jackass of a transportation who stood grazing at the Iron-Gate. "Look you all" said Mustave "that is my ride, his name is Konrad." Mustave's classmates found it strange that his family could not afford 30cents a day– for him to take the bus– but this was due to the fact that Mr. Levi has invested all the monies in the farming concepts of mount-7. In addition, Edith was not working.

All of the kids in Mustave's class had their optimistic speculations except for Kyro. Kyor understood all too well the boundaries that surrounded the statement; *making do with what you have in your possessio*ns.

This was one of the main reasons why Mustave and Kyor were best friends.

There was a spiritual connection and divine intervention that bonded them inseparable.

Kyro was a cushion that absorbed the negativity that always followed Mustave to class each morning. In return, Mustave gave Kyro his genuine friendship.

When Mustave sat down in his chair for the morning's lesson, Kyro caringly swats away the traces of jackass fur and shrubs that was imbedded into his uniforms.

"Thank you kyro" said Mustave. "I have a slice of pudding for you– but you will have to wait until we get to the canteen at lunch."

When Konrad heard the story that Mustave was planning to divide the pudding between himself and Kyro, he was beyond livid. Konrad immediately began chewing on his rope to free himself from the loop that was securely tied around his neck. However, the stealth of the carefully woven nylon-rope would prove to be time consuming and impossible to bite trough; but Konrad had the time and teethes to do this type of a job.

The early morning slowly proceeded behind the hour of noon… the lunch bell began to insert peace-of-mind as well as it brought all the kids into the canteen room.

Kornad, who was busy dismantling the knotted rope, also stood at hungers delighted attention– behind the confines of the big iron-gate, as if to say; *I am eager to devour my portion of mango, pudding, banana, fried-fish, hard-dough-bread and sugar-doused-lemonade.*

Kornad had a Clair view of what was transpiring in the canteen-room. Needless to say, that insecure livid disgusting feeling has returned. He immediately began chewing on his rope yet again. Konrad worked much fast and harder than he did before and eventually he was free. Konrad sprinted home through the village and sat down underneath the massive mango tree in total disbeliefs. Edith was surprised and wondered why Konrad has come home so early without Mustave.

Without speech to insinuate his lunch break dilemmas, Konrad was left sulking.

He simply could not complain to Edith; the one who packed the lunchbox for share.

While Konrad sat sulking underneath the mango tree, he could not digest or justify what he saw with his two big jackass eyes; Mustave not only forgot to give Kyro the slice of pudding he promised, he discarded the entire portions of lunch by himself and then went to sleep. When he was finally freed from his mid-day's nap; it was 4:25 pm, he closed the lemonade jar and his lunchbox– to face and even sadder note; where he'd left his furry transportation, all that was left was a piece of dismantled nylon-rope.

 Mustave was in shock— that his jackass of transportation has done such an unfair magic show and disappeared. However, with much energy to spare, Mustave took to the back track of his village and commenced his journeys home; on all cylinders firing at full velocity.

CHAPTER 17

Early 1 Saturday morning; Konrad, Mustave and Mr. Levi were destined to troop up the hills of mount-7— to continue the farmers rendition of replenishing the soils, in addition, add fresh food supply for additional growth and weed between the edges of each crop-beds– as if the vitality of the farm depended on it. Whenever that task was through, they would then poor water evenly around the roots to contain the moisture where it was most necessary. As soon as their tasks were completed, they would then make their way down from the mountain-7.

It has been more than a year and a half, since Mr. Levi had sewing his seeds in the soils of mount-7– and all that he has to show for his hard works and dedications were; a few heads of lettuce and plum sized tomatoes, a hand full of disfigured potatoes as well as rear discoloured water melons. *He could not understand why the rest of the seeds he planted had not yet blossomed or produced any form of fruits or vegetables.*

The seeds which came from the desolate-woodland of his forefathers were like trees that kept growing without remorse's or a prize. They were everlastingly tall– yet vibrant whenever the winds had arrived to carry the warmness to us all. The fruitless tress seems to always enjoy the windy-ride... but the fact of the matter was; as joy-struck as they danced in the wind, it was as if the roots of the fruitless trees carried a shame, a curse and a load of undoubting sins. They simply refused to produce a fruit or vegetable of any kind... *so it was imbedded in the thoughts of Mr. Levi– as he continued to hope for the day his fruitless trees would provide him with the ultimate win: Fruits beyond measures.*

Mr. Levi began doubting the fact that he'd taking on such an undertaking; thus, had left himself little to no-room for error or failure. However, the lack of produce of his labour tells a tale: that it was after all failure at its highest.

Villagers who optimistically criticized his adventure; felt loyally superior, in addition,

Saw his low rates of reap– as a victorious sing; that they were right to assume this would have been the outcome for Mr. Levi the former fisherman turned farmer.

They now had substantial evidences like ammunition, to mock and laugh at him even harder than they did before.

This was a major blow to Mr. Levi's ego, even though he pretended otherwise, there was so much bruises and scars to his emotion in more ways than one and what the eyes had beheld; every increment of trauma were slowly taking their tools on the physical being of his immortality and vitality. {As some of us may know; no man is an island.}

Patriotically Mr. Levi held is pains desolately inside.

Nevertheless, Mr. Levi commenced with his dedication to his farmland, his focus and his family. Whenever he heard the negativity of sarcastic villagers, he remembers his promises and commitment that he vowed to his family and apparition. In addition, he remembers the courtesy of the mayor and the kind heartedness of Mrs. Dubwise.

What they have done for him; was positive power that kept him striving for ***prospects of fruitions.***

Even though Mr. Levi was forbiddingly frustrated, today he straddled up Konrads' hamper with his farming equipments, his pepper mint tea and prominently packed his ambitions along for the ride.

At 5:00 am; the entire family were up to participate in this adventure. The sun has just made its way from behind the mist of mount-7. The sound of the local rooster resonated annoyances in the ears of each villager. The smell of fried-fish and hard-dough-bread crisping away on the hot pot of crackling coals, does justice to both Konrad and Mustave's appetites' and nostrils.

Konrad was preparing himself for what was a general disheartening routine. He was wiser about his salt and water intake in the mornings. He understood all too well that his salt and water combination made him a lot thirstier and extremely hungrier after a short period of time and he knew that he could not count on Mustave, to share his portion of what was in the lunchbox.

So Konrad devised a simple but cunning plan– to trick Mustave into thinking he had swallowed his handful of salt... And then Mustave came with Konrads' breakfast. "Good morning sunshine!" said Mustave to Konrad. Konrad immediately shifted his hoofs before the bucket went rumbling down. "*That was another close call.*" Konrad mentioned in the ass's language.

Konrad was keen on the kitchen and thought maybe today he will receive his fried-fish, hard-dough-bread, mango, banana, pudding as well as his fair share of sugar-doused-lemonade too. Kornad counted equal shares as Edith was packing the lunch intake into the lunchbox– but before he could finish assessing the correct order and quantity, Mustave tossed his handful of salt straight into the jackasses' mouth. Konrad pretend as if he was tastefully chewing the disheartening grains of salt and then swallow– but the minute Mustave headed back into the kitchen, Konrad spat the salt into the bushes and then washed his mouth with his bucket of water in total disgust. "Salt and water" mumbled Korand, "How belittling! Why is he never this gratefully happy to toss his lunchbox in my mouths direction? Sometimes I wish he would just choke on a fish bone; but that too has always failed... therefore let me down time and time again."

At 5:30 am, Mr. Levi, Mustave and Konrad began the journey up the hills of mount-7– 25 minutes later they disappeared into the mist that possessed the mountain. Eventually they'd made it to the farming grounds safe and sound. Mr. Levi assisted Mustave in unpacking his equipments from Konrads' hampers. When they were through with unpacking, Mr. Levi led Konrad into a shaded area and secured his rope to a nearby tree for the time being.

Before Mr. Levi began the day's chores, he released a series of sighs— and he then inhaled the fresh misty breezes that circled the mountain range.

Deep inside, Mr. Levi was slowly withering away. He'd kept a secret form his grandson Mustave, for far too long. It was slowly breaking his heart, thus, slowly he was beginning to succumb to Immortality.

On a brighter note, the presence of Mustave and Konrad inspired him to push on with the day's weeding and redistributing-earth process.

Back in the village, Edith took the time to do a day's worth of reflecting and sole concealments— before the men were secluded to return home. Edith began to reflect on a time in her life, when her heart was consumed with his loves and affections; a heart that once meddled with love was palpitating with miserable memories of his loss, pains and sorrowful disappearance. After what had happened, Edith refrained herself from the thought of ever loving again– that was something she could not consider nor comprehend. Emotionally her heart had stopped— when he disappeared.

Edith continued manifesting and concluded that it was time to confess to Mustave, what the truth was and how it all had happened. She figured that if she told of her secret, Mustave, would better understand exactly who he was and justify the relationship between him and kyro. Most importantly it would bring peace of mind to Edith, Mr. Levi as well as encase new insights into who Mustave really is.

The fear that Mustave would find out form a local in the village was weighing heavily on both their consciences' and they knew if the secret got out before they told of it themselves, there was no way to forgive their selfishness. Edith wanted Mr. Levi to be the bearer of all news; because he was the only eye witness to crawl away with his life in his hands.

How will little Mustave react to this secret? Will he be devastated, will it change his behaviours?

These were all significant things that Edith and Mr. Levi had to take into their considerations.

Emotionally Edith was a mess; tears had begun to pour out from the depths of a place where his dominance and love had conquered and rule. She wanted to see his presence for one last moment before she dried her sorrows of flowing emotion and before the boys returned home. Edith discarded her most precious memorabilia's of his memories in a secret location. Tucked neatly away from the discovery of Mustave, was a box containing a large amount of her most cherished memories!

Edith opened this box in anticipation of reconnecting with his love— she took out a picture and then held it up closely to her heart, as she stared off into the mist that circled mount-7. She softly whispered: "I am in need of your presence... your company... your assurance... your sweet charisma... your love... your friendship... your smiles and advices. I am in need of your touch. I miss you tremendously. One day I hope we meet again."

Edith held firmly to the picture for quite a while... when she was through, she placed the picture back into the box, replaced the lid and disclose of it yet again.

Her day of reflection was slowly winding down to its final moments. Edith then dried her tears and placed her sorrows in the confines of the box and returned to being: Edith the mother and chef of all that went into the lunchbox.

Behind the mist of mount-7, a pair of chosen doves protected the wealth that Mr. Levi had sewn into the soils of the mountain-7. They were guardian messengers sent to ensure: the gift was unearthed by the chosen owners. The two chosen dove were carrying and protecting secrets of generation themselves– as well as the secrecy of the hidden inscription. They were birds of mystery and magic, sent by Nostradamus and the chief of the Mayan people.

Eventually that day shall arrive, when their eyes of protection will be put to rest– but for now they have to be in total disguise of the mist that circled mount-7... with their entire undivided attention keen on the farming grounds. They maintain their guardian watch on Mr. Levi, Konrad and Mustave; as they worked between each crop beds.

Whenever Mr. Levi was at the grounds of mount-7, he felt a spiritual connection to his sorrowful past; In spite of his crops barely producing fruits and vegetables there were supernatural forces growing within– that kept producing his strength and courage to return to mount-7 again and again.

He knew something mysterious was underneath the mist of mount-7; Buried deep within the soils, he felt the energy whenever he inserted his tools into the earth.

Mr. Levi has been working all morning and he'd stop– to take a much deserved break— but suddenly he had a premonition that the Spaniard was rising form deep within. This premonition slowly turned into a feeling of déjà view; as if he'd been standing in his wheel house, he immediately heard the whispers of Melvin and Joshua– but as soon as the strange but powerful feeling came... it was gone.

Mr. Levi kept this to himself and went over to Mustave and gave him words of inspirations' and encouragements. "Hey son, you did well today, keep up the good work, one day you'll be in charge of all this" said Mr. Levi. "Thanks dad!" replied Mustave.

"I guess you can take a break and a bite to eat" instructed Mr. Levi.

Konrad, who was sound asleep, got up with excitement and began his survey of the lunchbox. Mustave could not wait to put away his gardening tools, to further put away what was inside his lunchbox. Konrad was pacing back and forth with all his hungered attention on Mustave, who was rapidly discarding both shares of fried-fishes, pudding bananas, mangoes, hard-dough-bread slices and sweet wash of lemonade.

Konrad could not digest the sight or taste of Mustave selfishness any longer; he stormed off the farming grounds with his unsettled animosity and acing hunger steaming from his nostrils... "Only a matter of time" Konrad murmurs in the ass's language... "Only a matter of time"

Konrad went far away from the sight and smell of the five curse lunch meal that Mustave has devoured all by himself.

Steaming with frustration, unsettling-hunger and unfair plays, Konrad was distressingly overwhelmed and demoralized— he'd suddenly lost his appetite, however, he swallowed a promise that he must repay Mustave for all his selfish unfair ways. Konrad knew that it was time he took a stand for what was his, what was right and fair; fish, pudding ,mango, banana ,hard-dough-bread and sweet lemonade were all for share.

Konrad disclosed of his plans in the center of his animosity and hunger. However, he was committed to instil swift action the very next time he made eye contact with Mustave's lunchbox. After carefully planning his method of reimbursements for Mustave, Konrad settled troubled emotion and hunger on a patch of hay and then he returned to witness Mustave sound asleep! While Mr. Levi gives his all around his crop beds.

The day was almost out of the suns guide, slowly closing upon night fall. They packed up Konrads' hampers and left the grounds of mount-7.

CHAPTER 18

Konrad was the most excited jackass in the village, when he heard that summer break was only a few-days away from written schedule to becoming reality. He could not maintain the misery of Mustave devouring his lunch portions any longer. So the news came as suitable relief, as he stood at the big Iron-Gate bounded by the nylon-rope that was knotted around his neck. Konrad was relieved to learn that he would not have to suffer this intervention for two whole months. Konrad would have chosen to munch on the fallen mango leaves that co-habited the base of his resting place; at the roots of the massive mango tree, where he founded peace and comforts; than to rather watch Mustave devour all that Edith had prepared and packed for both of their dwellings.

After all the belly-acing-turmoil's, there was a well deserving break in the schools schedule– for Konrad to exclude his humilities from the ordeals of Mustave and his lunchbox. Sub-curiously, Konrad has already detected changes in Mustaves' weight and body mass and it was arduously causing the hamper to bend way out of shape, In addition; causing strains not only in the belly and mind of Konrad– but also causing painful discomforts in his back as well. I guess it is fair to say that the act of selfishness has outstanding consequences' that gathered around the waits of Mustave, each time he'd devoured; 2 whole ripe mangoes, 2 bananas, 2 slices of pudding, 2 fried-fishes, 4 slices of hard-dough-bread and a sweet jar of lemonade– not to mention 4 hours of sleep to digest his feast.

Evidently, that day has come for Konrad to take Mustave through the village to school for one last time, until summer break was over. Konrad woke up earlier than he usually does... with the absolute proudest delights of inspiration; which included stability in his hoofs and jackass morals imbedded in his fur and waited for Mustave to carry his bucket of water and a hand full of disheartening salt.

The smell of fried-fish and hard-dough-bread were playing a miserable melody in the center of Konrads' fish delighted craved world– as Edith was preparing today's lunch for share. However, Konrad was not about to let the incredible smell of lunch, deter his set mentality; that today was that day– of the sweetest rejoicings of his self-worth's, thus, staying true to his locomotive end of the deal; so to speak. Mustave was equally very excited as well... today was his last day at school and Mustave was equally as excited that he would get to spend a lot more time up the mountain-7 with Konrad and Mr. Levi on this summer's break.

Not that long after Konrad was up and out of his bed of heaped mango laves, underneath the massive mango tree, Mustave followed in behind. Mustave's first priority was to attend to his four hoofed transportation; with his bucket of water and a hand full of salt.

"Good morning sunshine" said Mustave to Konrad... who took the initiative to meet Mustave half way between the mango tree and the kitchen. For once, both Konrad and mustve's mentality were on equal plains. Mustave gently placed the bucket of water precisely on the ground and politely gave Konrad his hand full of salt.

Konrad detected a sense of diligence in the aura and manner of Mustaves' attitude this morning... he could not help but let his cravings of edits lunch special guide his assumption to dissect the selfishness of Mustave, to identify if Mustave had plan to be this polite, thoughtful and genuinely generous throughout the day? Maybe then he could expect his portion of; fish, pudding, banana, mango, lemonade and hard-dough-bread.

Konrad drank his water and ate his hand full of salt optimistically, with high hopes that god has finally instilling changed Mustave for both Mustave's and Konrads' good benefits. In addition, hoping that it has been implemented in Mustave—» what it means to share.

Even though Konrad was optimistic about the lunch that was for share, he kept a watchful eye as Edith was packing equal amounts for share in the natural order: 2 mangoes, 2 bananas, 2 slices of pudding, 2 fried-fishes, 4 slices of hard-dough- bread and that jar of sugar-doused-lemonade. Edith then gave Mustave his regular advices, kisses and hugs– then waved goodbye as Mustave led his stubborn transportation through his gate.

The friendly feast that was neatly tucked away in the lunchbox was slowly causing Konrad a ton of grief... as he thought about the selfish suffering he went through this year. Konrad kept his head in the ground and carried his pride above his hamper, in addition, he kept the promise of repaying selfish Mustave; grinding between his teeth as if he was keeping the repayments promise sharp enough to dismantle Mustaves' craving jugglers or any cravings he had for that very matter.

Mustave was solidly full of more than just joy this morning; he was solidly filling up with the circumstances of his selfishness. The usually short 15 minute ride from his home to school was now taking kornad 35 minutes or more– because he had to stop and rest once or twice; because Mustave was getting heavier and heavier each time lunch break had came and went.

But today the journey took Konrad 10 minutes to get from home to school, he simply followed his excitements and it led them their quicker than before. Konrad wanted to get this day over and done with as fast as possible... he almost melted his iron boots on his quick journey. But he stood at the iron-gate in ease while they cooled; Konrad was enclosed in the smoke of his hot hoof and asphalts.

When Mustave pulled up on his four hoofed transportation, he belligerently parked it at the big iron-gate and secured it by the strong nylon-rope that was around its neck. But somehow Mustave had forgotten his lunchbox in the hamper and went on into his classroom.

Konrad thought to himself; that this was the opportunity he'd been seeking; to finally re-reimburse Mustave for his unfair share of the selfish deal. Konrad immediately began dismantling his rope, to set himself free; to make musical melodies of what was neatly tucked away in the lunchbox. The smell of the friendly feast gave kornad tons of inspiration– to chew through the nylon-rope as quickly as he could.

Konrad frantically tried to free himself, he was religiously hoping and praying that mustve would not realize that he'd forgotten his lunchbox as he chewed swiftly through the nylon-rope.

"How could such a glutton human being forget such a thing as his lunchbox?" Konrad wondered with unexplainable delights. Konrad had worked himself up a heavy sweat. However, the durable nylon-rope was proving to do its duty and honourable deeds; which were to protect and secure— much like the slogan that is visible on all police cars and jeeps.

The entire classroom could hear the grinding of Konrads' jackass grinders and molars at work through the window, so they all miscellaneously began to take their peeks; it was an historical event to the classroom. When Mustave finally stuck his head through the window, Konrad was a bite or two away from freedom... not to mention seconds away from devouring the delicacies of edits lunch menu.

Mustave, then noticed his lunch box inside kornads hamper and suddenly all hell had broken lose.

Mustave, jumped up from his chair and began to give chase to Konrad, who was escaping from his knotted rope at a thousand miles an hour. Konrad sprinted through the village swiftly; trying to elude Mustave, who stuck to his tail like a piece of dried jackass-dung. No matter where he went, Mustave was right behind.

"Konrad you ugly fuck, get back here!" shouted Mustave. "Listen here you craven jackass, stop immediately... my lunchbox is in the hamper. Now stop before it falls!"

"Kornad– Konrad... does my lunchbox resemble Mayan-bush or grass? You ass!

Stop...stop... stop!" But Konrad was deaf, dumb and blind to the cries and orders of Mustave.

Konrad and Mustave carried on this behaviour around the village... all that kept replaying in Konrads' mind was: the thought of Mustave devouring his portions of; crispy fried- fishes, pudding, mangoes, banana, and hard-dough-bread. In addition, sweet lemonade; each time musave sat down in the canteen. These disturbing thoughts fuelled Konrad to maintain his swift eluding tactics of Mustave. Konrad wanted to find a spot where he could sit and fulfill his famishing upon the labour of Edith's love– that was in the lunchbox. So Konrad sprinted up the hills of mount-7 with Mustave in full pursuit of his lunchbox.

It was surprising to Konrad, when he noticed that Mustave has not yet broken a sweat after masquerading around the village for more than 3-hours. The bad news was that the early morning breakfast of salt and water were beginning to take their tolls on Konrad. He needs to quickly get up the hills of moun-7– because he needed his share to eat.

Konrad knew exactly where he was headed on mount-7— it was a spot on Mr. Levis farming grounds; someplace where Mustave could not get to him, no matter how hard he tried; it was impenetrable to humans.

Konrad was in overdrive— as he dashed up the mountain-7– but Mustave was closely closing in on his tail. The mist of the mountain kept its watchful eye. The sound of Konrad hoofs; echoed as if an army of men were chasing its enemies.

Konrad entered the farmland utterly exhausted; to find Mr. Levi faced down between his crop beds. When Mustave came up on the scene, he cried "Dad...dad...dad!" But there were no replies... and suddenly the chase came to a sudden stop.

Konrad went up to Mr. Levi and used his head to roll him on his back. Mustave was on his knees with his jar of sugar-doused-lemonade, "take a sip"– he cried gently," what is wrong, are you ok?" The demeanour of their body language explained a troubling message. Kornad and Mustave began working together and figured out a clever way to get Mr. Levi between the hamper.

As quickly as they'd raced up the hills of mount-7– Mustave and Konrad found themselves in the ultimate race between the narrow pathways and time; to get back down the hills of mount-7 just as fast or if not faster than they had came up.

It was a sombre cereal mood as Mustave and Konrad raced off the face of mount-7.

Mr. Levi was unconsciously still-walled and he had not made the transition into the conscious state as yet. The state in which Konrad and Mustave had found themselves in told that the situation was grimly urgent.

Before Konrad and Mustave levered Mr. Levi into the spaces of the hamper, Konrad had bitten of branches from the fruitless trees, and placed it between the hamper, to act as a cushion for my Levi's body.

Konrads' immediate reaction was to quickly get Mr. Levi to the village hospital.

The sight of them storming down the mountain– has drawn a crowd. As word began to spread through the village, Edith received the news and raced to the hospital too.

A few tense minutes had passed before Konrad and Mustave showed up at the hospital's emergency doors, with Mr. Levi helplessly flopping between the jackasses hamper. It was a funny sight to many who had a moment to question and chuckle. Nonetheless, it was not a joke to Mr. Dubwise. He saw the seriousness of the matter and went to inquire and help.

"Konrad, is that you?" Mr. Dubwise Asked.

"I knew you were a special stable-mate! What is the matter?" He asked of Mustave. "What has happened?" However neither Mustave nor Konrad had an insightful response for Mr. Dubwise..."We found in lying in the fields of his garden on top of mount-7 and we raced here as quickly as we could." replies Mustave.

Mr. Dubwise requested immediate assistance and the entire hospital were put on special alert code blue.

Mr. Levi was rushed into the hospital emergency room, Konrad sat outside while Mustave sat nervously wondering– in the waiting room, waiting for a miracle... then suddenly his mother Edith has come to his aid and rescue. She rapped him in her love and comforts and asked Mustave what had happened? But only tears of replies were adamant.

Mustave was not only afraid but utterly embarrassed to explain to his mother; that if it wasn't for him chasing Konrad around the village to retrieve his lunchbox that she had packed for share; Mr. Levi wouldn't have been found! But he explained anyhow.

Konrad was sitting close enough outside and overheard the story Mustave was telling Edith and felt that he needed edits affections and condolences as well, not to mention his fair share of: crispy fried-fish, pudding, mango, banana, hard-dough-brad and sugar-doused lemonade too.

However, Kornad was proud to have carried Mr. Levi from the grounds of mountain-7 to seek medical attention; at the village hospital at which they sat waiting for news of Mr. Levi's conditions.

This early afternoon has already begun to prepare for the coming of darkness– the mist of mount-7 however, continued to maintain its secrets and guard.

No one in the hospital has yet to inform the family, the status of Mr. Levi's faith or the prognosis of his condition. As time went by they were clueless but filled with their speculations as to what may have happened.

Edith was deepened in a whirlpool of inconclusive desires; she could not tolerate another loss such as Mr. Levi. In that addition, she knew that Mr. Levi had not yet told of the secret to Mustave, so Edith began praying excessively that Mr. Levi would pull through for all their faiths sake.

Behind the walls, corridors and curtain; two floors above the waiting area, Mr. Dubwise and his emergency team, raced the clock to try and pull Mr. Levi from beyond the balance at which his life was direly hanging. Precious minutes and priceless moments has gone from miniscule intensity to sweat pouring hours— as they did what much and little they could to stabilize his vital signs.

It has appeared that Mr. Levi has suffered a massive heart-attack. The entire team of doctors in the operation room were all stunned and dumbfounded when they saw the condition of his heart. They speculated that the condition at which it was in; was like a quivered-prune left out in the sun to dry.

One doctor was beyond mesmerized and he suggested that if he was to guess the age of Mr. Levi by sight of his heart, he would assume he was a hundred and ninety-five years old. But Mr. Levi was only 50years young. The conclusion of the facts told that Mr. Levi was stressed beyond the limits humans were set to endure. But it was his dedication to live and work; encased with his dominant will powers that kept his aged-quivered-prune-like-heart beating after the doctors had messaged it back to its normal intervals.

For the most part, the situation was gaining positive attributes form the negative prognosis where it was.

The doctors have done all they could, the rest was left up to Mr. Levi to pull through.

"It was a miracle he'd survived!"

Mr. Dubwise and his colleagues were impressively amazed that Mr. Levi has survived because of the long time period he was unconscious and the time it took Konrad and Mustave to get form mount-7— to the hospital. "This man should have been tagged in the morgue."

The story of his mysterious survival threshold and the condition of his quivered-prune-like-heart made headlines around the hospital.

Curious, yet puzzled, Mr. Dubwise wanted to know if there was something that had kept Mr. Levi unconsciously stable for as long as he did.   Mr. Dubwise was adamant that there was something between the spaces of the hamper, which they've overlooked.

"it was just way too unbelievable— in all my years of practices, no one has ever been resurrect like he did or survived such an ordeal like Mr. Levi has done" he said to his colleagues with new found respects for the human's capacity to withstand.

He wanted to put his theories to the test and went back to find Mustave and Konrad to share the good news.   But he also wanted to see if between the spaces of the hamper had the miracle that held his suspensions pending.

—And there in the waiting room, Mr. Dubwise found Mustave and Edith in a sombre distressing mood. "Where is Konrad?" He asked.   Konrad, heard his name through the window; burst in through the door and stood to bare the news that Mr. Dubwise has brought.

"First", said Mr. Dubwise.   "I must inform you that we did what was physically and medicinally possible to retrieve Mr. Levi from a gravely place, he is presently stable, in recovery mode and alive".   Konrad, Mustave and Edith finally had that moment to relieve their intense stress levels at which they've been anchored upon.

"Secondly" he said "Konrad and Mustave you two are the biggest heroes of today!

I must commend you for your brave actions, which you've taken when you found Mr. Levi laying in the fields of mount-7... you were the biggest influences in saving his life.

And last and final: Mr. Levi has suffered a massive heart attack.

We are not certain how he is going to recover from this; his life may still be hanging in the balance!   All we can do is: hope and pray then wait for a speedy recovery.

He is in the intensive care's unit and we do advise that all family members wait a day or two before paying him a visit".

Mr. Dubwise reached into Konrads' hamper and took a piece of the fruitless-tree branch that was there and requested Edith's permission to conduct several tests for clues of Mr. Levi's survival threshold.   Edith was pleased to give her confirmation.   Mr. Dubwise then left the consoling family with a few means of encouragements and graces in his advice and hurried off to the laboratory to conduct his tests on the fruitless-tree branches, to verify if in fact there is a medical break trough.

Mustave, Konrad and Edith huddled close, to further embrace the good news... plenty of hugs and a warm welcoming embrace spoke with their affections; that they were pleased Mr. Levi was still alive.

CHAPTER 19

Mustave, Edith and Konrad, would have waited as long as their patience would endure to witness the head of their lives; Mr. Levi, hanging in the balance on his stilled-walled medical recliner, strung-up on high volumes of medications, plastic-tubes and vital-sign machines.

Two days had passed— since they were advised to let Mr. Levi rest before they paid him a visit. However, it felt much like 20-centuries combined with plenty of stalled millenniums as they withstood the acing pains of the uncertainty of Mr. Levis situation.

Moreover, their anticipation pushed them closer yet closer to the room at which Mr. Levi was in fragile rest and recovery.

The hospital had strict regulations and rule that prevented animals from curiously venturing into its germfree rooms and sanitized corridors; they were solely prohibited for fear of epidemic-contamination and the spread of unwanted diseases. With that been spoken; Konrad has hoofed his way between Mustave and Edith, to directly meddle in the presence of Mr. Levi, who was and still remains his provider and meaningful mentor.

Konrad was loyal with his friendship; ever since he ran to Mr. Levi, when Mrs. Dubwise opened the stable-door, many years before the prior intervention and not even the heavily guarded hospital door; could devalue the appreciation Konrad carried for Mr. Levi.

When they finally entered his recovery room, their highly driven anticipations turned sombre emotion into reliefs and joys; with a hart full of gratefulness.

Oh! What a cereal moment it was to encounter courtesy and respects... when a nurse opened the door to let them commence their very first visit.

"Who let this ugly jackass inside?" Asked a few caregivers; who were internally active with their patients? Konrad who heard the disregards on his behalf, hurry into the room before there was ever a reply to their inhumane inquisition. Soon after, both Mustave and Edith were inside the room too.

Mr. Levi was resting– but he was fully aware of their presence, he slowly turned his head in the direction where they stood and greetings were delivered with his expressional smiles; which did surprising justice to Mustave, Konrad and Edith, who had been waiting with the absolute unknown on his prognosis.

The welcoming smiles and welcoming demeanour has opened the door of hope as well as set the tone of the mood in the room.

Edith took his hand– as tears of relief poured down the contours of her face.

"Come!" Said Mr. Levi, "my son Mustave, I am extremely happy to have you in my visions as well as my arms" ...as he wrapped him tightly into his love and compassions.

"Konrad"...he uttered, "my stallion stable-mate." as he blistered with additional smiles.

"I am without words to express how grateful I am, to see you all presently at my presence. Just a few days ago, I never thought— I would ever behold you all again, so come my loved ones... let's celebrate to another day Livet together."

Then suddenly the visit was interrupted; when four security guards stormed into the room with 7-yards of the best nylon-rope, twirling in hand... seeking the furry jackass, who stood at Mr. Levis bedside.

"Grab hold of his big floppy ears" ...instructed one guard to another...

"And you grab its tale and you two secure its legs...Jackasses aren't allowed in this hospital... oh dear god it stinks like shit! Hurry let's get this over and done with soon, I am allergic to jackass fur" said one of the guards. "Not to mention he smells like rotten mangoes."

Konrad was ready and willing to put up a fight. He was not about to let four hospital security guards put a piece of nylon-rope around his neck, let alone; let anyone scar his heroic reputation.

Little did they know that Konrad was a bigger hero than the four guards efforts had combined.

This altercation drew many spectators into the hallways as they heard the camaraderie, eventually drawing Mr. Dubwise into the center of it all. Mr. Dubwise formally advised the guards that "Konrad had won his place and rights as well as reservation in the room like anyone else."

"Jackass or not, This jackass isn't going anywhere" he stated, "Konrad" said Mr. Dubwise, "maintain your position at will, while I lead these men away from disrupting the rest and recovery of Mr. Levi. This is intensive care, not a horse's pasture; this propaganda belongs out in the fields... now out immediately and shut the door behind you."

Mr. Dubwise defused the situation outstandingly firm, professionally and maturely and gave his regards to his resting patient— Mr. Levi. In addition, Konrad was left out of the nylon-nose that was surely about to be forced around his neck and hoofs.

When the jackass dispute was fully settled and peace had been restored in Mr. Levis recovery room, they picked on-up and carried on where they'd left off— before the four anti-jackasses -guards interrupted.

Mr. Levi placed all his affection and attention on Mustave, as he was preparing mentally to unfold his secrecy; as it had occurred when it did– but before he did so, he was commending his heroes for saving his life.

He was utterly speechless. However, his few kind grateful words spoke volume of Konrad and Mustave, who now had an uncompromising effect on his survival.

"I could not repay you two for the bravery and courage you've shown, however, for as long as I am granted the gift of life; you have my deepest respects and admiration." "Mustave my boy" said Mr. Levi "you've earned my honesty and what I am preparing to tell you may come as secret or even a major surprise... but I sincerely hope it does not change our relationship or change the person you are."

Edith listened and she felt all the increments of the secrecy pulsing through her heart as she too was preparing to follow the emotional journey with Mr. Levi and Mustave. She was prepared to lend her knowledge and wisdom whenever or if it was ever required.

Mustave could not comprehend that there was or could have been a secret kept hidden form him... because as far as his family life and families values; Mr. Levi and his mother Edith, were always honest to him... or so he was about to find-out— that there was secrecy in hiding ever since he was born.

As Mr. Levi digs deep to find courage and strength to deliver his confessions, his voice began crackling with pains more than anyone could imagine. He was literally reliving and revisiting a place and time; where he inherited a substantial amount of loss, sorrows and emptiness. It was as if, he was suffering those great abundances and his recent heart-attack all over again.

Nonetheless, he had to deliver his confession to Mustave, because his future depended on it... not to mention, no one knew for sure if Mr. Levi would pull through form the balance from which he was still hanging.

With limited strength and courage, Mr. Levi proceeded with all that was left within him... but before he was ready to begin his confession, Mr. Dubwise entered the room to conduct a routine check up.

"I am glad you are here to bear witness" said Mr. Levi to Mr. Dubwise.

"For what" Mr. Dubwise asked. "Maybe you should take a seat, this might take a while" Mr. Levi replied.

Mr. Dubwise was always a patron who appreciated a story, no matter the contents or what the story lines was, he was an honest listener; so he folded his stethoscope and drew his chair close to Mr. Levi's bedside, alongside Mustave, Edith and Konrad, and became part of what was set to transpire.

"I clearly remember the events as it unfolded— as though time was a caption set on repeat. I've done my share s of reminiscing and concluded that I am the one who made that irreversible decision; that carried our enthusiasms and then drifted us with one objective; to re-enter the dock yard with our bounty of stacked fish-pots.

I can still feel the wind of the sails— as it drifted us upon the unsteady seas, to stock and retrieve the riches of the deep.

But the worst acceptance of it all was that: on that faithful day, there was nothing to gain; instead, I lost my missions in life as a captain, a fisherman, a father and a friend.

I've lost my will to live— when I lost my son and Joshua, his very best friend, my best shipmates and deck hands... but their bravery and willingness has allowed me to maintain through outstanding pains.

However, described Mr. Levi... my *survival is to tell the tales of what meanings are secretly coded in our given life ...* in addition, said Mr. Levi, I survived to hope and spread their legacy, their strengths, genuine love and immeasurable willpower."

Tears had already soaked the atmosphere; as the sadness of the ocean waves shores on both Edith and Mr. Levis darkened complexions. The depth of sadness was beginning to resonate through the room— and caused Mr. Dubwise to unfold his stethoscope and placed it around his neck; in position, just in case he felt that Mr. Levi and Edith's vital signs had sank any deeper than it was. Moreover, Mr. Dubwise was officially overly interested to hark on the story Mr. Levi was preparing to deliver.

Needles to say, he felt that this was about to get a lot more interesting than he was ordaining for.

Even Konrad the furry jackass has repositioned his massive ears in perfect location to eve's drop on the conversation.

Clueless but totally clued in, Mustave opened his mind to this secret session. All that he could have done was pay perfect attention to the words of Mr.Levi, just like Konrad, Mr. Dubwise and Edith were doing.

Mr. Levi was sobbing internally; the pulses of his vital signs were also throbbing tremendously. "Are you willing to subject additional stress on your heart and continue with this?" asked Mr. Dubwise. "Just a minute" replied Mr. Levi to Mr. Dubwise... "I must comply and continue even if it means my life if tipped of below the balance. I will not live with this any longer– let alone die with the truth of matter."

Edith could be seen nodding, as if she was agreeing to his commitment to follow through with the story.

"I must honour and preserve Melvin and Joshua as brave soldiers of this world."

Silence was the nature of edit's dispositions, she knew it would have been difficult to fester up such a secret, however, she was presently deliberating that it may not be the time or place. Like wise said Mr. Levi to Edith, as he read the fine-prints of her thoughts.

Mr. Levi's persistence, told that he'd been manifesting this moment a thousand times or more. You could tell by his guilt ridden tone; that he was at wits-end: with, withholding this information. Therefore, he was overly ready to set his secret free... therefore, freeing his conscience; thus, replenishing his honesty and admiration for Mustave.

Before Mr. Levi began his next sentence, there was a slight pause— a moment in which he was lost; as he was reliving a daunting task of revisiting the haunting of what had happened. He was baffled and fumbled all his words.

It was obvious to those who were listening that his phrases did not deliver sensibly. His tongue was tied, dried and heavy. In addition, his emotion was drawn.

"I have taken full responsibility for my actions, it was entirely my fault. I led those young men astray and I should have been with them too.

However, said Mr. Levi, there must be reasons for everything, my survival and their demise."

Even though Mustave was clueless, he was beginning to feel a connection in the secrecy as if, he was as important to the secret; as each word that was spoken by Mr. Levi. Mustave was finally succumbing to the intense sadness that was present; he lowered his head, to show his emotions were forthcoming; as he gazed upon sadness of lost.

The sorrows and sadness in the recovery room was heavily strung, it slowly began escaping into the corroders of the hospital, literally escaping through the locked doors and sealed windows. The rhythmic beeps which came from the vital-sign-machine increased then decreased– as Mr. Levi was transitioning from reliving the nature of his dismays then back into this present reality.

Nevertheless, the strength and courage he need, was only a thought away for him to rely on; to further tell the story exactly how it had happened...

Mr. Levi poetically expressed severe regards, acing sympathy and deepened gratitude's as the attention level of Edith, Konrad and Mr. Dubwise could be disrupted by the drop of a dime... the silence in the room vibrated the spectrum of the stethoscope as it curled around Mr. Dubwise's esophagus, it was tangibly deafening.

Presently, the dialogue of the compelling nature of the secret unfolding; reversed the moment as it was, when they drifted beyond the safety of the dock yard, into the deepened wide body of oceans and brought the minds of; Konrad, Edith, Mustave and Mr. Dubwise into the captains wheelhouse of Mr. Levi— as he reclaims the begging of what was his ultimate end.

"A few days not too long ago" he whispered audaciously, as if, it was just a few days ago, "the local fishermen consulted their fishing calendars, to determine the shifting of present tides and the guide of the moons eyes, so that gratitude and good-luck will reward their bounties, when they had set then return from their sails.

The festivities of this overwhelming consultation had caused the fishermen to gather at the local pub-house, in an astounding number of eager fishers of men, who demonstrated their unsatisfactory caused by the season's drought. With flaring tempers constantly increasing, the brewed potion of the local distillery fuelled their peeking testosterones.

It was as if, fishes and crabs had grown straws and leapt out of the ocean and left the friendly currents on pause; while the fishermen frantically decipher a reasonable cause. Their nests were solidly dry. The growth of cobwebs had taken full ownership of one to all fish-pots. Propellers were hesitant to rotate!

The anticipation of desperate fishers-of-men had escalated; causing random vandal acts as a result of their frustrations.

Needless to say, without the fishery of the seas to settle confrontational minds as well as compensate the local fishermen, untamed hostilities made the village economically and emotionally unstable.

Fish for the most part was most important above other niceties'...not only was it a way of income: the villagers prefer sea-food above anything else that was on the foods chain.

However-the-more, fish and crabs had decimated form the villages reefs, outbound as well as neighbouring shores.

It has been many months since the water gods had caused the fishermen's drought but there was sings»» that the circling seas, was once again daring to be reaped."

Mr. Levi the seventh was the best fisherman in the village. He out-fished his competition time and times again. He was proud to state that his son and deckhand Joshua, were closely the only two worthy predecessors»»to the highly fisherman's throne. Mr. Levi had been fishing for uncountable years, which stemmed from his early childhood-days and adolescent-nights spent upon the tides.

He later turned his hobbies into an honourable way to provide, in doing so; he continuously settled the matters of mindfulness.

He knew the rocky reefs, the fishes and crabs, the nautical circling shores as equal to knowing his own child. He understood the weather, whether to stop and set anchor or procrastinate the shift of the glowing moon, before he sent his fish-pots to the oblivious dark and deepened matters of the seas.

His judgments of sardines' and crabs were astounding to Joshua and Melvin. They wanted this incentive of knowledge themselves— **but patience was the key to prosperity and their success; as they slowly but imminently will understand it in the lessons and the unearthing— along with those who were the chosen's**

Fishing was flowing in his blood; as if it was caused by the strong pull of the ocean current that dominated the seabeds around the village-shores and more.

Mr. Levi had planned to set his sails and lift his anchor a few days earlier than the others; that were eager to make a ***golden*** catch out on the unsteady seas. Even though he was cautioned by his fisherman's calendar not to toy with the powers of the seas, he was poised by the still of the midnight moon; that the words of his calendar were simply dust residing in a fine tomb.

He was positive his guiding intuition would lead him into prosperity; where amberjacks sardines' and crabs were bountiful in the cargo hold of the Spaniard, when they'd returned from the drifts of the seas.

Scouring the vast distant of oceanic views, he felt a connection between his intuitions and the clouds that combines into ocean blue, as if a positive voice told him to get going on the journey and fish like he always does or even push himself and shipmates just a tad harder than he'd done before.

So he wasted little time gathering his fishing equipments, necessities' and belongings; pots, lines, hooks, baits along with his container of peppermint bush, fruits and hard-dough-bread, Diesel-fuel and enthusiasms'.

This encounter of the seas was all confirmed and written down in his mental obituary. Mr. Levi was alleviated to disembark the ties of the dock yard, ominously ready for fishes of ***gold***.

"Melvin was always ready and willing and very much eager to participate in the family's traits too... Whenever Joshua, he and I had drifted beyond the village-shores, to reiterate the quota of fish-pots containing; crabs, mussels and valuable sea oracles, Melvin was at ease, most of all; he enjoyed the challenges in which the seas had to offer..

Nonetheless, it wasn't always boredom aboard the Spaniard, it was often sails of rivalry in sunder-competition, between father and son, best of friends, in addition, love and naturalness of a father teaching his son, who was finding his manhood– as he was strongly following in behind his father's footsteps»»of top-class fishers of men.

Melvin was not just a brave, inquisitive, intelligent, fast learning young stallion; who did not fear the deepest nautical element or death, ever since his mother had died, when he was 17 years old. He was so much more and worthy of his father's love and proud praises.

Nonetheless, he was traumatised by his mother's sudden passing but he found peace upon the seas; when we drifted to and from shore to sunder, to retrieve the catch that waited in the fishing pots.

Melvin had a lot to be thankful for– when it came to the circling ocean. Even though he lost his mother, he gained wisdoms, patience and balance; along with his notable courage, out on the open ocean. The current which flows up and down, had drawn Melvin's fear and deception apart... therefore creating inspiration; in co-placement, his unique perfection to overcome the unthinkable... thus mastering his craft to be called top-class fishers of men.

Melvin's popularity had grown; as his journey into manhood went up the masculine ladder. Melvin had grown from teen to handsomely keen... a defined man—with respect for live and his goals. Thus; he always remembers the words his mother had told..."

...Give respect to others and lead with insight controls...

"Behind the humble-handsome-stallion Melvin– many women would follow but one stood above them all. Edith was the apple of Melvin's eyes— not to mention she held the key to his everglade heart; tenderly in her loving arms.

Romance had grown out of their connections, passion was adamant when they shared affections. It was hard thought to see them in a lover's separation.

Whenever it wasn't fishing season, Melvin and Edith, would spend considerable amount of time together. They both understood the dangerous line: between the village flats and the currents, which causes nausea between family and fishermen. It is important to note that Melvin's career was obviously adding negative and positive chemistry, in addition, credibility to the relationship that they shared. Edith appreciated Melvin, more and more whenever Melvin and I had returned from the gruellingly long fishing season.

It was as if, she fell deeper in love; but then roes higher to loves appreciation highest level, whenever the Spaniard has set anchor at the village's shore.

Ever since the fishermen drought had scared last year's fishing season, Melvin and Edith had that opportunity to spend and spread love proudly in their romance— at the cost of the peril season.

It would be very understanding to all– that our quota of fishes was at a major loss.   Nonetheless to say, their time spent was that of laughter, growth and in-describable awes..." *{'Unknown to the two: a bun was at rest in the oven'}...*

"Immediately after Melvin and I, had gathered all of my fishing equipments formally in the fisher's man pile, then checked the charts that our shipping vessel would be stocked with all that was required for the season's run; Melvin quickly discarded himself with his emotions tucked underneath his sleeves, he sought the residence of his darling Edith, to bid his farewells.

When Melvin finally stumbled up on Edith's house, dark had already settled; with little time to waste or spare, Melvin settles in comfort with his prized jewel Edith.

As the night continued to consolidate upon lover's romance, Edith prepares a feast; to showcase her appreciation. She kindly puts aside a reasonable portion for me as well. it was strange to find sardines' and lobsters in any kitchen utensils– at a critical time as what had occur upon the village, but Edith was quiet the saver and tonight's occasion, she had a secret stash of seafood on the menu.

Edith had certainly worked up a wonderful storm in the kitchen, with a secret ingredient called love... but in the back of her thoughts; she was presently succumbing to her moment of withdrawals... as a sour taste of sadness sinks into the reality that Melvin was hours away from a {seamen departure}which interning, meant that beyond the curtains of their farewell-romantic-show; both Edith and Melvin would have to give all that they had inside— as well as between...{just between the sheet}... as the hours of dark stood up with the early mornings greet.

The sound of lover's appreciation grew beyond the door of romance— the night grew evermore silent and still... so followed the movements that were at play.

Edith and Melvin retired, thus; falling asleep, with an awesome encounter on their minds which should last until his return!

However, before they knew it: the common roosters were there to remind that sleep was for the absolute jackass-don-lazy!"

As that time grew closer and closer; it kept pulling Melvin, Mr. Levi and Joshua, closer yet to the village shore.

"Melvin's egos were nun deterrent– as like with most men; he cared a bit more to venture out to sea, than to see that Edith was drowning in a ocean of sorrows and sadness. But Edith was a true trooper and she knew this moment would have come! Needless to say, it was nothing new. Before the two was tentative, thus ready to get up out of bed, Edith stared into the deepest depths»» into Melvin's eyes, then she whispers: "you are my life, my companion, my lover and best friend..." she uttered gently "you are everything to me, be safe on you seasons' trip. I cannot imagine what life would be without you."

She smatters him in plenty kisses, then coiled him with the very best of wishes and when she was through, she asked of Melvin: "can you please return to me soon?!"

Melvin then reciprocated his affections by wrapping Edith into a snuggle hug. She was warming with his reflectional tenderness, which transcribed the sincerity of his gratitude and love.

"My darling Edith" said Melvin... "I love you much more than measures would show, you are my world; and if you would kindly give me your inner spirit, I would kindly yet proudly and boastfully take you out on the nature of the seas' as my angel guardian."

Edith was overflowing with his manly seductions– as she remembers why she was so in love with her prince charming. As they fell into a moment of genuine companionship they assured, then reassured each other; that their love was securely tied into a knot, tied to each other»» forever.

CHAPTER 20

At 5am— Melvin, myself and Joshua, would set our sails out in the abyss of the ocean mist, thus, leaving behind our despairs— as we rode the continuum drift's; to regain that confidence that was broken by the unfriendly seasons drought.

Melvin's anxiety had created tons of excitement for this seasons fishing run.

Empathetic to say; he would rather spend his time out on the open blue, rather than be stuck around the yard; twiddling his thumbs— because there was not much else to do.

As Melvin made his way from beneath the comforts of Edith's intentional caresses, his passions for fishing led him to a known pathway, to retrieve his best friend Joshua; he was a well established deckhand on my vessel; the old gal Spaniard.

At approximately 4:35 am— Melvin and Joshua's excitements collided in the front of his yard, they both has had ongoing thoughts and contemplated about this encounter for months now... so they wasted little time in the yard. They took pristine honours and the liberty to be the first to enter the dock-yard, where they knew their captain Levi, would soon follow.

The agonising 15 minutes it usually takes Melvin and Joshua to reach the dock-yard; took them only 7 minutes to get there today.

They wanted to make a defined impression on their captain, so they took the incentive of stocking the empty fish-pots in their kept location.

After the shelves and storage-cupboards were neatly stacked form ceiling to floor, it was time to reorganise each bait-lines, bowies and mussel-baskets... then manipulated the order of all that was undone on the ships worthy list... so in the presence of their captain, all that were left to do was; climb aboard my old gal Spaniard, then tooth my horn, retrieve my anchor and be on the way... to reclaim the title of best fishers of men of our village; before any other fisherman had the chance to daringly do so.

As eager and anticipated as Melvin and Joshua were— it could not have added up to the amount of anxieties that had captivated my humbleness and desires to be out on the open ocean; doing what I loved.

Long before the common roosters had sounded the lazy man's alarm, I was up at the crack of dawn. But for some strange reason, I lingered around the yard with the difficult decision of: should I or shouldn't I?

Eventually, when the conclusion was set it stones; the sun had already stood above the village and I was late and seemingly the final being to reach the dockyard.

I was contemplating the decision— as I paced back and forth in the yard, wondering if leaving before the official star of the season, was in fact the correct thing to do?

Should I refer to the advice of my fisherman's calendar or would it be to imposturous to set sails this early? conditionally would it be best to wait for the official start of the season, to be joined by the other fishers of men; just in case we ran into trouble out on the open seas, help would be close enough per say? I asked of myself as if the trees in the garden would provide some form of insight to my curious inquires.

The thoughts of the last few uncompromising months caused by a peril seasons drought had placed myself and the other fishers-of-men in a critical decision making dilemma.

Somewhere in my thoughts and decision making process, I knew there was a slim margin for competition.

No-one in the village was absolutely 100 percent certain that all the fishes and crabs had returned to their channels and spawning trough... so, to be the first fishing crew to gather what was there for the taking, would only mean our efforts will reward in victorious laughter's and not of a quota despairingly quoted as a loss.

Is this just my eagerness taking toll– thus, causing me to lose my fisherman's control?

I asked, as I paced upwards then down in the front of the yard.

Then I remember the true spirit of fishers of men; is to take the imminent risk and return with bravery, courage and complimentary crabs and tons of fish.

With satisfactory in my decisions to continue with the fishing conquest, I quickly got all my sea destined belongings together and sped out of the yard, in the direction of the dock-yard. When I finally made the grand entry into the dock-yard, I was modestly surprised by the presence of Melvin and Joshua; diligently securing the fish-pots in their kept position.

"Hey dad slept much?" Melvin asked

"We almost left without you!" Joshua implied

Morning boys, what bad news brought you two out so early?

Their excitements had settled my current worries, therefore, reassured»» that maybe this was a just decision after all.

When I got onto the Spaniard, I noticed that all was done on the list of things to do. I was happy, alleviated and exceptionally pleased.

You two definitely out-did your selves today, "thanks" replied Melvin and Joshua.

"However, we felt this would be inspirational for this season run and beside our old lady could have done well with a bit of TLC— here and there; more like everywhere" implied the obvious deck hand Joshua. You two are too kind and thoughtful. I replied. You just might receive that raise you've been inquiring about.

Joshua and Melvin were chuckling with the news in raise.

Well boys this is it, another season will begin momentarily. Will you two put away the food in the pantry, so we can begin on this fishing adventure?

"Most definitely, we shall get to it at you moment's notice."

"I! I! Captain" Melvin and sergeant-deck-hand Joshua chuckled.

Being the captain I was, I was ready to lift all anchors and Bouie from off the dock ties but before I did so, I unfolded my charts to plot the course before we made off on another maiden voyage.

When I began plotting my courses and finishing grounds, I lucidly remembered that on the last fish run»» 7 of our pots were left behind; due to a storm that was closing in on the Spaniard... so without further- a-due, we chose to leave them behind and return to the safety of the dock-yard, with a notion that we would return to retrieve the fish-pots when the weather had prevailed.

I knew that chances were slim that his fish-pot would still remain in that very position, due to the strong pull of the currents and the forces of previous storms that have passed. However, I was willing to take a gamble on their recovery nonetheless. In addition, 7 pots of fishes and crabs would add an incredible amount to my lost quota; which would make up for lost wages, due to the season's drought that had descended on all fishers of men from his village.

Finally, I decided that it was well worth the gamble; so I placed a marker on the location at which the 7 pots were left. In addition, I knew that in that very location, sardines' schools in large numbers as equally to overgrown amberjacks... so therefore, this would be an excellent place to set high-hopes inside a few of our enclosed fish-pots.

Melvin and Joshua had returned from the pantry's duty glowing with curiosity and additional excitements than ever before.

"Where to, captain?" They asked. Ship mates, we are headed into the flats of the Bermudian triangle; to retrieve our posts and do a bit of sardine fishing. If luck is more than willing, we shall inherit more profit if we obtain extra amberjacks, I replied.

Both Melvin and Joshua were not surprised; they knew exactly why we were headed into the Bermudian triangle.

"Dad, do you at all believe our pots are still there loaded with sardines' and crabs?" Melvin Asked. Son, always learn to lead with your optimism, I will be able to give you solid conformation when we get there and they are fully erected from off the seafloor... I replied."

Moments prior, Mr. Levi proudly powered up his massive-9-cylinder-diesel-engines, with set course and destination fully comprehended in his mind and on his charts.

It was time for the Spaniard to power out of the dock-yard. The condition and forecast was accurately perfect for sailing at that particular time of year. The predictions were that it would remain fishers worthy for another 4 months— before the stormy season began. In addition, the moon had intended to give a guiding light at the presence of night falls.

"At approximately 6:15 am— on that beautiful Sunday morning; Spaniard the fishing vessel steams out of the village harbour, into the abyss of open seas.

Gradually it disappeared beyond the distance»» until it was no longer visible keen."

CHAPTER 21

Even long after the tides that brought another display of the whispers of the noble sailors had settled onto the shallows of the dockyard, captain sir William Levi the seventh floored his medal and accumulated maximum knots, to maintain his sails into a distant of open blue and freedom driven breezes; with his objectives in mind as well as on charts»» to make the very best of deploying this early on a seasons run.

The Spaniard held and maintains her mercies– as she protected her precious crew of: 3 men.

She was stocked with enough fuel and food to last at least 6 months or more. It pushes onwards»» as it powered over a wall of unfriendly rising wave, before it then balanced to maintain its set sails.

Nevertheless, her ballasts contained the correct quantity of sea water that assisted in dampening the sea driving ride– as each set of waves came and went discreetly on by.

On board the ship, spirits were high, at last the 3 men were out of the village doing what they loved to do; fishing and spending time together. It is modest to say»» this was their way of life, not by choice but by a higher celestial divine.

Back in the village; all the other fishers-of-men were clueless that Mr. Levi had once again snuck out of the harbour to set and retrieve his fishing pots before anyone else had that opportunity to do so. This cunningness of his was one of the reasons why Mr. Levi was the best fisher man around. In addition, Joshua and Melvin were worthy to be called the best deck hands / fishers-of-men themselves. Their collaborations had turned out the highest paid fishing quotas for several years and they are yet to be beaten.

A great sense of pride drove them further yet closer to the sardines' fishing grounds with the help of the massive-9-cylinder-diesel-engine.

"It's only been an hour— yet if feels as if we've traveled and ocean over. On the other hand; it seems as if we're not moving at all— it just feels as though we aren't moving fast enough," said Melvin. "I felt that strange premonition too" said Joshua. "Are we almost there yet captain" asked the boys? Mr. Levi was proud and polite with his replies, "deckhands– I suggest you two put aside your egos and excitements and get some rest– because 1014 miles of open seas stands between us and work, so settle down and enjoy the ride. If all goes well, we should be there in a matter of time. And that is more than plenty of time to rest those eager bones and muscles of yours— because when it is fishing time; best bet we are fishing boys. Buckle up and saddle down."

Not to say that Melvin and Joshua needed instructional insights on their egotistical criteria. However, sometimes we all need to be told what is meaningful and just.

In addition, a word of wisdom that is in our absolute best interests\ a good advice so to speak; should arguably be a systematic welcome when needed.

It seemed as if Mr. Levi had shrunk their excitements to a seamen's snooze. it also seems as if his words of encouragements had left him with the captains logbook, with a long list of things to do all by himself— as Melvin and Joshua found deep aspirations' for the soothing motion of the ocean, which cradled them deeper yet deeper to dreamland and beyond.

Mr. Levi thought to himself... "Finally some peace and quiets, dam these two can definitely talk up a storm"... he uttered to his beloved co-pilot: the Spaniard.

"You sound beautiful old lady! when we return to the dockyard, I promise you old gal a full restoration from keel to stern, engine room to bow, bowies and anchors... just you and I.—After all these years, you've earned it. You've been very reliable at my services beck and calls."

"How about a new paintjob... Hey old gal... New pistons for power!? A new rudder and propellers!? You name it and consider it yours!"

The sound of the Spaniard's engine relayed a soothing message, only one in which a captain could understand– as if the conversation was well understood by captain and boat. Mr. Levi increases the throttle, which created a vibrating burst of speed. The gauges at his controls showed; the Spaniard had clocked an impressive: 45- Knots, knocking Melvin and Joshua around in their peaceful sleep.

A few hours had passed— and many distantly miles had been logged in the captains log book. The drifts of the ocean remained the very same.

A group of dolphins has joined the Spaniard into the sardine chase. Nonchalantly, Mr. Levi didn't seem to mind his new competition and surprisingly he welcomed them because he saw them as many worthy pairs of eyes and tons of fishing knowledge.

The sound of their echoed whistles had drawn Melvin and Joshua from beyond a peaceful place.

"Slept much" I asked them sarcastically? "I almost made it without your concerns, thanks for your appreciated help boys; now hurry on back to sleep."

"Hi dad, are those dolphins following us again and form where?"

"Why didn't you wake us up captain? You know we enjoy the dolphins' giving chase" said Joshua.

"You two looked to peaceful, I could not have led myself to intervene on such a comforted parade; maybe next time, thanks anyway."

A series of sarcastic chuckles came from Mr. Levi.... as Melvin and Joshua scraped away the remaining rest form the corners of their eyes.

Intrigued by the playfulness of the gathering dolphins, Melvin and Joshua became instantaneously wide awake and settled to enjoy the oceanic view at the marine show. Without a doubt, the dolphins had taken up all the attentions as they continued playfulness; while maintaining the chase with the Spaniard.

This was more than good news to Mr. Levi, this was just the kind of conformation he needed– that the fishes and crabs had returned to their know positions. Mr. Levi immediately took hold of his binoculars and counted the numbers of dolphins that were in the area. He knew that a large count of dolphins meant positive in the fish count. On the contrary: a lesser numbers of dolphins meant; they were in an unpredictable dilemma as all the other fishers-of-men were in.

With all his experiences and knowledge's of fishing, Mr. Levi knew that there were wiser fishers-of-men who knew a lot more than he did; these fishers-of-men were born inhibiters of the ocean and surrounding sea floors. In addition, Mr. Levi was willing to put the dolphins' in the captains chair; giving full control of his wheel-house, knowing they would lead him into schools of fishes and crabs that awaited abundantly in pairs.

Finally it seems as though there was a bountiful reward waiting for reap– because of the decisions he had made to be off on the open seas; simply because his dolphin count was surprisingly staggering. As Mr. Levi continued his count, dolphins kept joining the convoy form all visible angles, which kept increasing his anticipations' to begin setting and retrieving his 7 abandoned fish-pots.

Melvin and Joshua were too caught up in the actions of the swarming dolphins, to notice that they had already made way into the Bermudian triangle, sometime ago.

Mr. Levi began to scan the horizon as instructed by his compass and charts. He scours form left to right, north and then south; for visual markings that would lead him exactly where he had left his 7-fish-pots.

From out of nowhere, he spots two of his Bowies that were tied to his fish-pots. "We are here shipmates, time to do some fishing"... he added with excitements.

The playfulness of the chasing dolphins had gone completely still. Their echoing calls had gone silent— their movements and presence had vanished without a trace... Which could only mean; they were hundreds of feet below the Spaniard feasting on the sardines schools. Mr. Levi slowed the Spaniard and lowered his anchors and prepared his crew to star operation early-bird.

Mr. Levi and his gang Melvin and Joshua has transformed from dolphin spectators into top class deckhand\fisher's of men in an instance. All hands were eagerly ready on the deck of the Spaniard.

"Our first objective was to secure the pot-lines, then intercept the Bowie; so that they could retrieve the fish-pots from off the ocean floor. We all took pride in teamwork doing just that.

Melvin has secured one of the lines onto the spool; that reeled the pots onto the Spaniards deck. Judging by the squeaks and time it took the fish-pot to reach the surface, I was absolutely positive it was full of fishes and crabs. Be ready to pull her in boys, she seems heavy."

"We are on it captain" replied Melvin.

"I, I captain" uttered Joshua.

"The sound of the revolving motor assured us that this pot was insecurely heavy.

Here she comes! –When the pot finally made it onto the deck; Joshua, Melvin and I were seemingly filled with joy.

The fish-pot was stacked like a sardine-can, filled with sardines, amberjacks and crabs.

We began cheering with the circumstances of the first catch of the day. After a quick rejoicing moment, we emptied the pot and then manoeuvred to repeat the process as the second pot-line was secured around the spool; that contained another one of our fish-pot.

This time around, I took my turn and casted out the lead line— bull's eye, I uttered with innocence; after tossing it overboard. See boys, this is how it's done... it just proves that the old man's still got it. I began to pull on the line as fast as I could and then secured it around the spool of the revolving motor.

The sound of the squeaking motor began its familiar cries– as the pot slowly rises from off the ocean floor– but as fast the rope began to accumulate around the spool; all movements suddenly stopped— the motor was no longer working.

Get the grease gun Melvin; it must be another loaded pot that caused the motor to stop. Then suddenly it began to move. Never mind, she's up and running again.

But before I was able to finish my sentence— the motor stopped dead in her tracks. Check the lines josh, is there enough tension? "Yes captain stiff as an anchor."

Then there was movement. "She's a tease" Joshua implied. "She certainly is" replied Melvin.

For several minutes the faulty motor continued its anonymous activities; working then not working.

There wasn't much we could have done but waited patiently until the pot was visible at the surface. Eagerness had taken tools of my consciousness... therefore, I applied a generous amount of grease, in hopes; it would speed up the process. However it did not have a positive effect on the faulty motor.

25 minutes had passed by— as our anticipation turns to frustrations. Even-more, the sun was hot as an igloo. Neither one of us had a tactic or a reasonable solution that would inspire the faulty motor to retain its proper functionality.

"I think I see it breaking the surface" ...cried Melvin. "Yes I do" said Joshua.

The post was in range. We decide to pull the rest of the distance using our bare hands.

On the count of three, pull with all your might– was my verbal command for them to do.

"I! I Captain, on your command!" Ready?

Melvin, Joshua and I began the strenuous haul; the sounds of agony took over the deck of the Spaniard– as the strain on the rope caused the motor wheel to squeak unbearably. There must be over a thousand pounds of fishes and crabs in this pot boy's.

"It sure feels as if we've hit the mother loads of crabs" said Melvin.

"Thank god, I am fit and strong!" Said Joshua... "This pot must be filled with crabs covered in tons *of gold*"...he chuckled— as the squeaks of the motor wheel significantly increases.

You keep dreaming of gold and one day you might wake up in the harvest of a goldmine, I murmured jokingly.

Visibly the pot was already on the surface of the ocean, it created a small amount of displaced waves; as it was under the force-pull of: Melvin, Joshua and my strengths.

The sight of the pot on the surface has brought a dose of strength combined with inspiration, which inspired and strengthen us three men; to work like machines, to pull the pots aboard the Spaniard.

The combined efforts of Melvin, Joshua and I, manoeuvred the heavy pot to the starboard side of the fishing vessel... all that was left to do was: to place the rope around the manual crane and crank it aboard.

Melvin was the closest one to the manual crane, he quickly but precisely encased the rope between the winches and held the crank handle– while me and Joshua came to lend our helping hands.

We are almost through– I shouted, as if subliminally instilling a last burst of courage to finish the job. Ready? —Let's get this done and then we can take a well deserved break.

"I, I captain" replied his deck hands Melvin and Joshua. "Let's do this captain!" Joshua said.

We all began to crank the handle, in the clockwise direction, the rope that was between the winches stiffened with each rotation.

Finally, the pot was aboard the Spaniard. "aaahh!" —a breath of relief– rushed from out the lungs of each man; who had done his fair share of hard work for the prolonged moment. Melvin, myself and deckhand Joshua, were all relieved that the fish-pots were finally on deck and can be counted for as recovered.

However, tiresome and weariness has left us in no mood to be standing much longer, so with the mission completed, we sat down to regain our breaths– as well as our composure. We were literally overworked!

We were so exhausted that we immediately ran into the wheelhouse to sit down, Joshua was the last to enter the confines of the captains domain. Rejuvenated by his gasps of freshly inebriations; he was left with the task of closing the door behind him and that was when he noticed— there was a significant difference between one of the containers and our distinctively built fish-pots. What have we pulled aboard the Spaniard was more an unsettling mystery than anything else.

"Ah! Captain" said Joshua... "I think you need to verify that situation»» that is sitting on the deck." as he pointed»» at the wooden container that was in the direction in which his fingers were directed.

What was that skipper, I asked? "That is not one of our pots" replied Joshua empathetically. "What do you mean" inquired Melvin and me?

"Look for yourselves" ...Joshua replied. And just like that the situation on the Spaniard had changed.

How could I have been so distracted not to notice? — I ask myself, it must have been my exhaustions that caused me to pay little to no attention to what we had hauled aboard. Melvin was at a loss for words— as he stood gazing at the wooden box that was on the deck. However, the more time we'd spent concentrating on the wooden box, our curiosities rose. It definitely seems as if— it is from out of this world, not like any fishing pot or container I'd ever seen before.

"Well!" ...said Joshua, "that may also explain why it was so dam heavy, without lingering doubts, I think we've found a pirates treasure chest" ...he added positively. "Let's hope it's neatly preserved with *gold* and precious *gems* and not filled with fishes and crabs."

Melvin was eager to dig into the find, therefore, the curiosity escaped from his mouth; "so are we going to find out what's inside or just stand here and take mental photos all day long?" ...He chuckled.

Ultimately that decision was solely a captain's decision. At this moment my heart was pumping with finder's curiosity too. However, I held my composure solemnly solid; just the way a captain should.

Nevertheless, I was more than obligated to find out what was enclosed inside the wooden container. The big wooden box has suddenly become the center of affection as well as the center for attentions.

As time went generously with the forceful currents, I could not settle my ongoing thoughts and eagerness to obtain conformation of what was inside the wooden container. Being a good decision maker and a captain, it wasn't too long of a debate; before I've decided whether I should let this strong feeling of inquisition lead me into the container we'd found– or wait until we've returned to the dockyard before the contents of what was inside settled our minds.

Ultimately, the pressures of Melvin and Joshua, weighed if favours of seeking the unknown contents that hides inside the wooden box.

Well fellows, let us put our curiosities at rest... I am going in. I began to pry the lid open with a piece of pipe that was loosely residing on the deck of the Spaniard. While I held firmly to the rusted piece of shipping pipe, a thousand or more thoughts of what could be inside ran into my mind. I was hoping treasures of outstanding values and **golden** coins; that are beyond a dollar's worth. But at least– if I was to open the container and find a dozen fishes and crabs, it would add confidence to our enthusiasms... therefore, increasing the fish count that was already in our pots.

When the lid of the container was finally free form where it rested; a blinding light flooded our eyes.

Melvin, Joshua and I, placed our hands above our faces to try and shield our sights from the bright blinding gleams that took over the environment.

With caution; I placed the pipe aside and then stuck my right hand inside the box, to retrieve the objects that possessed such a magnificent blinding gleam. When my arm was reverted from inside the wooden container, I was holding onto the lost Mayan crystal skull; that should have been delivered to our village by the 3 Mayan sailors, many centuries ago.

The sense of the situation captivated the power of silence—not a word was uttered; all movements had stalled to a still-disbelieving-moment.

The crew of the Spaniard found ourselves puzzled, in addition, curious more now than we were before. Then suddenly my world became a mass of loss– and darkness, Melvin and Joshua along with the Spaniard, crystal skull and box was swept away by a gigantic killer rouge wave.

For all strange reasons and intuitive purposes; I am the only one who survived.

I woke up on the villager shore, with the pain, the sadness, the misery, lingering questions and memories of Melvin and Joshua."

"Mustave" ...said Mr. Levi sombrely... "Melvin was your father, my son.

You are biologically my grandson. I am sorry", explained Mr. Levi with sadness in his abbreviations. "Joshua was his best friend; Kyro is the biological son of Joshua"

Mustave could not process the information that he'd been receiving fast enough, to conjure up his replies– if any. His jaw was literally on the floor– as he thought beyond the story... he was searching to find reality beyond this world and more.

Mr. Dubwise and Edith, were steps behind Mustave, as they too tried to place the pieces of what was just told form start to finish, in a genuine prospective.

It was just too touching and way too much to decode and decipher.

The chimes from the vital sign machine began to sounding excessively. Mr. Levi's vital signs were descending beyond normal too rapidly... until the chimes went completely dead. The moving green bar that was on the screen was flat-lined_____.

So too»»»» was Mr. Levi!

Moments before the chimes erupted, he took his last intakes of life's precious commodity and memories; he then closed his eyes, he cleansed his consciousness and he then returned to join the apparitions of his dreams.

CHAPTER 22

Words could not have manifested or measure the pains and perils both Edith and Mustave were feeling– ever since Mr. Levi has digested the last memories of his family; to carry with him to the underworld of apparitions; when he departed their domain countless times ago.   Needless to say, Mustave and Edith, picked up the overwhelming sorrows and bandaged their visible scares, then slowly moved»» on– as life naturally allows the existing ones to do.

Mr. Dudwise became a positive dominant figure as he grew significantly closer and compassionate to Mustave and Edith. He even had a sweeter spot yet for his furry friend Konrad as well.

Life was technically tougher– without Mr. Levi not around to carry the weight of the family. It was even tougher for Edith, not having an income. In that regards, Mr. and Mrs. Dubwise committed their genuine-giving-gratitude to Edith, whenever she was in need. The sour part of that news is; Edith has found the bull's-eye in the jackpot, of the neediest patron in the village.

Nevertheless, she would not go beyond a pity to neglect her self-worth, Edith would always multiply and magnify her blessing with words of prayers; sent to the gods of hope and the needy.

With that said, there was a massive downsize of the portions that went into Mustave's lunchbox, his breakfast bowl as well as his supper plate.

Overwhelmed with the untimely loss of his grandfather Mr. Levi, Mustave had quite a load to digest off his mental table. There were many thoughts that ran consecutively through his mind– often at times; Mustave would sit and relive the story his grandfather has told of his father and Joshua.

Whenever Mustave was in thoughts of his father, it brought him one step closer to his mystical realities and all that is buried beneath top-soils.

Mustave was missing his grandfather dearly. He was often left feeling down and oppressed by his emptiness, his need and his wants of Mr. Levis directions and companionship. He wanted that positive emotion– he once felt when Mr. Levi was around. He missed the early morning adventures, when they hoofed up the hills of mount-7– to the farming grounds.

Mustave was tremendously missing Mr. Levis advices... but if Mustave had learned or kept anything from his grandfathers teachings; that positive sense of restored being he'd been searching for will come and return to stay forever.

Konrad on the other hand, has been feeling this emptiness and misery quite the same as Mustave and Edith.

However, Kornad had a unique way of finding peace of mind in the memory of Mr. Levi; by wondering off up the hills of mount-7– to the farm grounds, which remained the very same as Mr. Levi had left it; fruitless yet hopeful.

The playful breeze that circles the crop beds whistled that soothing melody that came from the depth of Mr. Levi, when he would attend the roots and stems of his crop beds. It sounded and felt as if he was still present; however, it was simply delusional thoughts in the mind of Konrad.

The mist of mount-7 covers the farmlands heavier and heavier each time Konrad had come to re-live the memories he once knew.

In honours of his gratitude's, Konrad would spend his moments up the hills of mount-7 gathering earth around the fruitless trees; with his hoofs, as if he was commemorating the tradition and legacy of Mr. Levi. In addition, it seems as though Konrad had a sensitive intuitions that was leading him to and from the hills of mount-7– to gather earth around the fruitless trees of Mr. Levis garden.

Konrad would work the entire farmland, until the guide of the sunlight was no longer present; he did this continuously— under the watchful eyes of the mist.

When Konrad would return home, his four-furry-hoofs and body was filled with the earth of mount-7. He then went underneath the massive mango tree and waited for the next morning's bucket of water and hand full of disheartening salt.

While Konrad sat braving the discomfort of darkness underneath the massive mango tree, he thought tremendously about; how much he wanted Mustave to capture a positive resolution that would inspire and lead him up the hills of mount-7— to help preserve the vitality, by placing earth around the crop beds of the fruitless trees.

If there was a voice that spoke the loudest at the gods of hope and needy; Mustave, Edith and Konrad, had won the number one spot in that category. The question was, were the gods of prayers, hope and the needy, lending their listening ears?

—And then came another sunrise, to inspire the many lives that surround the village.

The sound of the ruthless-roosters at this morning's light; displays a sense of urgency that all walks of life should triumphantly raise, at the sounds of their annoying trumpets.

The busy bees make haste to devour the fresh nectars of the blooms; before the humming birds were ready to reset their ongoing restless snooze.

Before too long– the hustle of the early morning was consuming with activities of each villager. The mist of moun-7 instantaneously descended onto the village. Visibility became poorer; as it was free of guard duty from the reserves of mount-7.

Mustave could scarcely see the pathway, which led to the massive mango tree, as he carried a bucket of water and a hand full of salt for Konrad.

The mist of mount-7 purposely consumed Mustave, as he tried to make his morning journey.

The fog like substance began circling Mustve– as he placed the bucket beside Konrads' hoofs.

Both Konrad and Mustave, heard the ruffling of feathers and the flopping of wings. Suddenly the misty fog disappeared. Konrad was startled— as he and Mustave, witnessed a pair of white dove ascended into the house. The pair of dove dashed by sporadically as Edith was preparing breakfast on: the hot-pot-of-crackling-coals.

Edith was surprised but thought little about what had happened. She figured that they've mistake their flight path and flew out the window that was at the back of the house.

The smell of fried-fish and fresh hard-dough-bread crisping away on the hot-pot-of- crackling-coals; sent shivers down the spine of Konrad, as he digested his bucket of water and hand full of salt.

Even thought the loss of Mr. Levi has brought on an unbarring sense of depression; the smell of fried-fish and hard-dough-bread has always brought along a refreshing revitalizing portion on hope. In addition, the smell of Edits breakfast brings into the prospective of Konrad; a sense of negativity that has grown from the dislikes of Mustave's inability to share. Therefore, as Konrad swallowed his portion of water and salt, it is a mouth full of love and hate... a sense of needs and wants— equal portion and the fact that he's yet to receive his end of the deal.

This morning's bucket of water and hand full of salt was chewed up with bitter sweet dilemmas.

Konrad made his promises, that one day in his lifetime»» he would repay Mustave, for his harsh and crude treatments; for his inability to share.

Konrad swallowed his mouth full of bitter sweets along with his promises: that it didn't matter if Mr. Levi was dead or alive! Little did it matter if Mustave was drowning in an ocean of sorrows; Mustave needed to be taught a lesson!

It was obviously apparent, that this was a touching situation, which irritated Konrad; whenever Edith was preparing a meal around the hot-pot-of-crackling-coals.

Ever since the passing of Mr. Levi— Mustave has not yet set an anchor or his foot into his classroom, let alone place his weight around the hamper that sat on Konrads' solid structure; due to the situation that came with Mr. Levis death.

Financially, Edith could not afford to send Mustave back to school. In addition, Mustave was stressed beyond his limits... therefore, Edith agreed that it was best if Mustave took time away from school, until his mental capacity was stable enough for further learning's.

The wound of his grandfathers passing remained fresh-as-could-be! No matter how much time had passed; the loss of Mr. Levi was always a teardrop away from his memory.

Mustave was finding little to no peace-of-comforts being away from school and he was missing his very best friend Kyro, more than words would explain.

Edith decided that with her last 27 dollars; she would re-enrol Mustave, for one year. Mustave was excited to return to Scholl, to live his life like a regular boy should.

Konrad on the other hand had mixed emotion about this venture— seeing that the lunch portion was dramatically cut in half.

Konrad already understood the outcome of the routine that aggravated him to chew himself free from his nylon-rope at lunch break recessions.

Konrad was selfishly imminent, that Mustave should remain home for another 7years! He saw no harm or fowl-play; if Mustave sat around the yard and brings him the regurgitating breakfast of: water and salt... at least there was no discrepancies' of him doing such a meaningful task...

Today was a day of rejoice-full return— as well cunningly very predictable to and for Konrad.

After the two dove had flown into the house, Mustave came in just a few moments after, to ready himself for his long awaited return to his classroom.

Mustave could not contain hi excitements, he was so eager to fill Kyro with all his dilemmas. In addition, he could not reframe from telling him about the sad stories of his father Melvin and his best friend Joshua. Mustave was beyond a happy place– when he thought about sharing the news with Kyro; that Melvin and Joshua were best of friends– just like he and Kyro are.

Mustave was returning to school humbled– but he had a deeper connection with his best friend Kyro. So he hurried into his two bedroom house to change his attire.

When Mustave stepped into the room to change, the misty substance that was circling him in the pathway to the massive mango tree, just a short while ago, was ever present and circling him quite the same as before.

Suddenly the window to his right swung open. When Mustave looked at the window he saw the two feathered white dove that eluded his vision earlier. They were peaceful and friendly, ***they carried a scroll***.

The two dove flew the ***scroll*** up to Mustave and placed it in his hand, they then flew out the window.

The incident had caught the attention of Mustave, but his exciting return to school was the most important thing on his mind at this particular moment.

So Mustave placed the scroll into his bag without much concerns and quickly changed into his school uniform.

While Mustave was inside preparing to leave for school, Kornad has firmly cohabitated at the kitchen steps; where he had a positive bull's-eye -view of what transpiring in the kitchen. Konrad was making certain, his detective skills were put to the test– as Edith placed the meager portions inside the lunchbox.

Edith was finally thru with preparing the lunch portions and she decided that even though her portions were drastically downsized, Korand and Mustave should not and will never go hungry. With that said, Kornad drew even more closely to the kitchen door, to verify if there was a small portion put aside in the lunchbox for him too.

Edith began placing the items in the lunchbox more optimistically than times before... she felt helpless about the small portions– that she was packing in this natural order as follows:1 banana cut into two half's.

1 mango sliced evenly down the middle.

4 ounces of pudding equally sliced into small bites.

4 slice of fresh hard-dough-bread.

2 teaspoons of butter!

1 crispy fried-fish cut into two equal pieces; one head and a tail for share.

Half jar of sugar-doused-lemonade and a separate jar of fresh spring water.

When Edith was finished packing the contents into the safety of the lunchbox, she looked directly at Konrad and mentioned that; "there is always a portion inside of this lunchbox for you Konrad."

Konrad was more than overwhelmed with the news he'd just received. However, he was speechless to inform Edith that he was yet to taste the delicacies, which she'd been preparing on the hot-pot-of-crackling-coals ever since he could remember.

Konrad was certain– that today was that day; for him to taste the portions of the lunchbox. What Edith has told him before she closed the lunchbox, was like a musical symphony– filled with inspiration, which added fuel to an already brewing fire in the belly of the beast; Konrad.

Konrad has vowed that he was going to get his portion, whether it was given to him by Mustave or not.

Before Konrad could finish his thought— Mustave came into the kitchen to retrieve his lunchbox, his mother's love as well as her words of advices and encouragements.

Konrads' bitter sweet emotions were already at its highest boiling point and the sight of Mustave caressing the lunchbox from off the kitchen table, sent steams raging out the jackass nostrils and ears; of the furry jackass Konrad.

Konrad, slowly and optimistically counted his steps as Mustave led his transportation thru his gate and then trough the village– to the big Iron-Gate, at which he was bounded by a sturdy piece of nylon-rope. Konrad became significantly irritated, which increased his appetite of hunger– but Konrad braved his hunger and stood restrained by the strong nylon-rope that stood guard around his neck. He waited ever so patiently; to hear the lunch-bell– at lunch breaks recession.

In addition Konrad kept a close eye and his ears in the classroom, where he had all his attention pending on Mustave, as he made every move and sound.

Mustave was the topic of all conversations— as the hour-hand spun slowly and closer to lunch break. Everyone wanted to know what had happened to his grandfather Mr. Levi and how he was coping with the death of his provider and mentor.

Mustave adjusted perfectly, even though he'd missed several months of school, he connected with the work that he was given and opened up to his teachers and classmates.

Mustave was ready to overcome and move beyond his darkest days of loss.

It was a positive attribute; to see Mustave finally smiling again and interacting with his peers. Mustave and Kyro sat on the same bench as the teacher instructed the classroom but their attention was drawn into the story of the seas— as Mustave was whispering to Kyro the story; the very same way as he heard it from his deceased grandfather Mr. Levi.

Kyro was taken by the story... and he too has come to terms with the loss of his own father Joshua. It was a significant loss for Kyro, but the new connection he was feeling from his father's past; added a positive degree, that climbed even higher than before in his friendship with Mustave.

He also felt that there were divine spiritual connections between their genuine friendships. They were now bonded (BFF) best friends forever, by tragedy and faith.

In addition, bonded by *the ink of the inscribers feathers!*

Mustave spent his entire morning explaining to Kyro, all that has happened in his life from the last time the two had sat down in class like this... to the ordeal with the two dove earlier this morning. He told Kyro, about the farm that was up the hills of mount-7 however, the teacher interrupted the conversation between the two briefly, so Mustave told Kyro that there was something he wanted to show him at lunch. In addition, they could continue the story when they got into the canteen.

Konrad, who had all his radars in the conversation has mistaken what Mustave was whispering to Kyro— and thought Mustave, has once again offered Kyro, his portion of lunch when they got to the canteen... therefore, Konrad began to make waste matter of the strong nylon-rope that was around his neck. But before Konrad had worked himself up a sweat, he understood that Mustave, said to Kyro; they would continue the conversation in the canteen... not that he was giving Kyro, his portion of lunch in the canteen.

Konrad relaxed and lowered his racing heart beats and raging tempers.

As soon as Konrad was fully calm and settled, the melodies of the lunch bell set his entire being on high alerts. This was the moment they'd all been waiting for.

The sound of the lunch bell, reminded everyone that hunger needed a bite to eat; included Konrad, who was standing upright on all hoofing fours, to verify if Mustave was heading to the gate»» with his portion of»» banana, mango, pudding, hard-dough-bread, fried-fish and sweet lemonade.

Unfortunately, Mustave went on into the canteen, eagerly to show Kyro the scroll that was deposited into his hand, by the doves that came from the mist of mount-7.

When Mustave and Kyor sat down to investigate the matters of the scroll, a piece of paper fell onto the floor before it was open. "You dropped something" said Kyro to Mustave. "I got it said Kyro." Kyor picked up the loose papers and then placed it on the canteen bench as they sat down. "Thank you Kyro" replied Mustave.

When Mustave and Kyro sat down around the canteen bench, their hunger was overtaken by the strange symbols; that were all etched into the scroll... but neither of them had a slight interest in the contents of their lunch boxes. However, fuelled by the genuine nature of Edith, Konrad was exhaustingly interested in his»» portion of what was in the lunchbox.

Konrad had his visual cues on the lunch box»» where it was sitting untouched, graciously wrapped-up in the brown paper bag»» inside Mustave's school bag.

Immediately, Konrads' in-tuned suspicions began to divert his hunger.

This was not like Mustave— not to devour both portions by now...» after fifteen minutes had passed, Konrad was surprised that glutton Mustave, was not already sound asleep; in a coma-tossed-zone.

It seems as though the contents of the scroll and papers, had all their attention pending. Konrad began hoping and thought that his»» prayers are finally answered.

Twenty minutes had already accumulated yet there were no attempts or advances made at the lunchbox.

Konard was relatively certain that changes had come and it was only a matter of time before the gods of hope and the needy; will send Mustave to aid the hungry furry jackass with his portion of; crispy fried-fish seasoned to taste, hard-dough-bread, sweet lemonade, pudding, mango, lemonade and banana.

Back in the village, the old whispers of the Mayan sailor's descended inwards— as the waves of the ocean anchored its presence into the village, then into the souls of each villager once more.

The locals believed that whenever it was noon; it was important and very traditional that everyone should have a bite to eat. It was said that the three Mayan men of the seas inscribed it into the philosophies of the village and villagers. Thus, even them that stood on all fours in the fields of hay, obeyed by grazing on the greenest of grasses and fragments of clay.

However, Edith was trapped between her sad realities and her past— as she sat around a steel oven, without a trace of the ever present hot-crackling-coals; with a concerning demeanour that spoke loudly evasive.

Edith was in a distressing revelation– the point of the matter was; she'd given the last meal to Mustave and there was nothing in the reserves for dinner.

There was no solution to overcome the empty problem; no fish to fry, no banana to sooth, not even a crumb remained in the bread basket and the sugar jar was absolutely empty. The flour container became crystal Clair— all that remained in the coal-pot were residues of burnt ashes. All the mangoes had disappeared away from the massive mango tree– as a result of Mustave's daily double.

All that was left were a hand full of sour limes and **Golden-lemons**.

The sour taste of edits realities mimics the rhymes of the **Golden-lemon** and sour limes as she tried to contain her sadden emotion.

Nevertheless, the acidity was too much to overcome; many mercies washed away in all of her tears– as she digested the sour taste of today's and yesteryears realities.

Edith was feeling the difficulties and strains of life more negative now than ever before. Shame and necessity was a heavy load to accept, Edith had her responsibilities pending yet there was emptiness all around her circumstances. Just when she thought life was promising, things have gotten excruciatingly painful, unbelievably imposturous and scornfully demoting.

"What am I to do?" –Edith asked the gods of silence. "You've taken away my Melvin, then Mr. Levi... my friendships... my love... my rock and my providers and left me with darkness and a heart full of pity... not to mention a mountain full of fruitless trees."

But to her cereal surprise– there was no replies to her inquires. The mist of mount-7 began shifting above the mountain range, bringing hopeful insights into the mind of Edith, as if it was the answer she'd been searching for.

Edith believed that the gods of silence»»»»hope, pray and needy was speaking to her; by shifting the mist above the mountain-7.

"Was it a sign that there was harvest in waiting to be reaped?" she asked herself silently. "At this point in time, if I went up the hills of mount-7 there was more to gain than I had already lost."

Edith immediately rid herself of all negative thoughts and feelings, then gathers her lemons and lime and decide that there must be fruits and vegetables on Mr. Levis garden. Even though it was a fair distance away,

Edith filled her water container... then hurry away to the hills of mount-7»»
in search of dinner or uncertain disappointments.

Back at the school yard, Konrad was still standing mystified with an
everlasting burning hunger sensation in the depths of his pit; yet weary and
intrigued to know what has captured the interests of Mustave and Kyro.

Nonetheless, Konrad was exceptionally gratified, that he was not yet
annihilated form the lunch portion. After all, the lunchbox was yet to be
opened and or tampered with.

Therefore, it was an insight filled with waiter's inspiration; that inspired the
furry jackass, to stand upright on all hoofing-four– just a while longer.

Mustave and Kyro, were both in a state of forensics– as they sat around the
canteen bench encased in the mysteries of the scroll as well as the contents
that were written on the papers that fell on the floor moments before.

Before too long, Mustave and Kyro, had discovered just what was written
on the papers: it clearly reads as follows; Mustave, Kyro and Edith, were
beneficiaries of mount-7 and all its properties and contents that reside
there.

Mr. Levis land titles and deeds included the names of Mustave, Kyro as
well as Edith. Whatever that meant to Kyro and Mustave; it was very
uncertain.

However, the uncertainty of the scroll and title papers would only pull
their attentions towards»» mount-7; literally pulling them into what was
rightfully theirs.

Kyro and Mustave packed up their titles paters, deeds of ownerships and
ancient scroll, to venture up the hills of mount-7... just because they were
boys ruled by curiosities. They decided that it would be a cunning idea,
to sneak away from school and spend the remaining afternoon at the
crop-beds; redistributing earth around the fruitless trees, in honours of
celebrating the news they found on the titles and deeds»» because they
were rightful owners of mount-7 and all its contents.

Insomnious by hunger, Konrad sent mental messages to Mustave and Kryo;
that the lunchbox was to accompany them up the hills of mount-7... some
way or another Konrad was destined to eat his bit of the lunch portion.

Mustave was eager, to finally introduce his furry jackass of transportation»»
known as Konrad to Kyro.

When Mustave and Kyro showed up at the Iron-Gate, Kyro understood
all too well the epic tales of the furry jackass and his unethical annulment
behaviours, of past encounters witnessed; when Konrad would chew
himself free of his nylon-rope that secured him to the big Iron-Gate... and
then disappears to the comforts of his massive mango tree.

With differences set aside, Kyro met Konrad with his open arms and open
mindedness.

Mustave introduced Kyro to Konrad... "This is my jackass and Daily
transportation" he mentions... "Yep, ugly as a duck and stubborn like a
mule. His name is: Konrad."

"Hello transportation unruly" said Kyro to Konrad.

Konrad took a serious liking to Kyro immediately... or was it simply a
hoax to lower his suspicion, to get what was in the lunchbox some way or
another?

Was Konrad about to use the joyful moment as bait; to fish the lunchbox
away from Mustave?

Konrad was very elated that Mustave and Kyro wanted to venture up the
hills of mount-7 to redistribute earth around the fruitless trees.

It was something dearest to his heart... and Konrad though– it was a sign
of the gods of hope, silence and the needy answering his cries of getting
through to Mustave.

With that said, there was plenty of time remaining for them to do a lot of
work as well as male to jackass bonding.

Konrad carried Mustave and Kyro on either side of his hamper, proudly
up the hills of mount-7...with his watchful eye and mind at all times in
perfect perspective of his portion in the lunchbox. Stability strength and
positive promises were signs that resonated from the strides of Konrads'
steps, hoofing up the hills of mount-7... harmonized by»» the friendly,
happy laughter's of Mustave and Kyro.

This was more than a prayer answered! This went above and beyond the expectation of the gods them self.

This adventure sounded quite the same as when Mr. Levi and his troop, would hoof up and down the hills of mount-7»»with a hamper load of fruits, food and vegetables– but it was a new army on patrol; Konrad, Kyro and Mustave.

Alarmed by laughter and the solid thumping of Konrads' hoofs, the mist of the mountain gave a watchful eye as they came up the mountain, joyfully as they'd ever been.

...And up»» the mountain they came... Kyro was in awe; breath taken by all the lush greenery and cool breezes that weaved between the trees and then beneath Konrads' hamper.

"This is spectacular and truly refreshing" said Kyro. "I could spend all my free time here, just relaxing under the secrecy of those trees."

"It gets even better" said Mustave. "Once we get to the crop beds, the breezes begin to sing into your ear." "That is way too cool" replied kyro. "Your grandfather must have felt this also and that must be the reason why he bought the entire mountain-7."

Mustave replied silently intelligent, however, he smiles to show he understood what Kyro was implementing into the subject.

"The closer we get up the mountain" said Kyro, "one can begin to feel the presence of the mist at your finger tips and taste a mysterious but magical presence at the tip of your tongue. *It almost fells as though we were journeying under the wings of caring heavenly doves.* My intuition is telling me that there are more here to discover than what meets the eye."

Something was manifesting itself through; sight, smell, touch, taste, sound and the environment that was picked up by Kyro.

"Mustave" said Kyro; "I just got this premonition that we belong here. In addition, there is an ominous connection that riddles between you, me and the compounds of the deepened earth. This isn't a coincidence why we are here! It was meant to be."

Mustave could not understand where Kyro had gathered such lucrative thoughts. However, Mustave agreed that this was a special place like no other indeed.

Konrad was hoofing up the hills of mount-7 so hard that the vibration of the hamper shook the scroll loose form the safety of Mustave school bag.

"Hold on Konrad" shouted Mustave and Kyro "we drooped something."

kornad slammed on his four-hoof-brake-pad, made of rigid harden weather proof jackass ivory; sending Mustave and Kyro in a head's dive.

Mustave landed on top of Kyro. The good news was; the lunchbox was safely secure in the hamper.

Mustave and Kyro, got up form their disposition at the edge of the shrub garden and rid themselves of any evidence of the fall.

When Kyro picked up the scroll, he noticed that a large part of what was shaded resembles the contours of the hillside at which they were presently standing.

In addition, the bottom half of the mountain had a ***golden*** tone to its appearance.

The more he studied the scroll, it became apparent that what he was holding in-front of him was a map of mount-7... but he could not cipher the meaning of the strange hieroglyphics symbols that was written and etched.

It was tremendously intriguing to them both. ***They wondered if there were anymore discoveries to be unearthed before they were ready to leave the mountain that was rightfully theirs.***

Konrads' excitements drove him into the playful path of Mr. Levis crop beds, leaving Mustave and Kyro to continue the reaming journey on their own four cylinders.

Konrad began tossing earth around in all directions to show he was extremely happy that his hoofs were once again in-touch with mount-7... but hunger was speedily approaching, faster than Mustave and Kyro were.

After 10 minutes of earth full play, Mustave and Kyro finally showed up on the farm ground... to do their shares of unearthing, weeding and redirecting the earth pile around the fruitless trees. Konrad was pleased to be within their presences, he had already devised his plan to devour his portion of what was in the lunchbox.

Konrad waited for the calculated opportunity to disappear with the lunchbox.

Kyro gave his undivided attention to Mustave and Konrad, as he was given the formal farmland introduction quite the same as They'd received it from their beloved grandfather, the very first time they planted hoofs and feet on mount-7.

"This is it" said Mustave. Konrad kicked up a hoof full of earth at Kyro, to show his appreciations. In addition, it was a cleansing gesture as well as a welcoming ritual.

"This is where my grandfather, Konrad and me worked, then played and spent most of our times; that was when he was alive. Yep, we planted all that your eyes does see– but the funny part of it all is»» there isn't much reward, a few heads of lettuce, honey tomatoes, a hand full of disfigured potatoes and a hamper load of melons form time to time... but as you can see with your own two; those trees that dominates the farmland they never produce, nada, nothing! They never grew any form of fruits or vegetables. I've given them all the same nick name: ***the everlasting fruitless trees.***

Now that I think about it, my grandfather treated them with the same care and respects as the vines and trees that produced fruits and vegetables, which brings me to this inevitable part of my story»» we best begin by redistributing fresh earth around our fruitless tress." "What purpose does doing that solidifies?" Kyro asked.

Kyro was overwhelmed— as well as overcome by the introduction Mustave has given him, not to mention a head full of earth that Konrad kicked in his direction.

More so, he was taken by the many acres of fruitless tress that had to be tended and cared for. But before they began, kyro had a question for both Konrad and Mustave.

"Did you grandfather ever say if and when the fruitless tress would produce and if so what would the fruitless trees provide— as a reward of the farmer?"

"My grandfather once said that it is unjust to question mother earth, mother nature and the mother of all irony, he just appreciated the fruitless tress quite the same as the potato stalks, the tomatoes stems, his lettuce roots and his melon vines and continued to weed and water the roots of all his trees in his garden. In addition, ***he said that sometimes we need to follow»» the roots like we seek to reap the harvest of all planted vines and stems"*** Mustave replied with wisdoms outlined in his replies.

With raw courage and wisdoms implemented in the mind and consciousness of Kyro, he worked between each crop bed and vines with tremendous appreciations, inspirations and a genuine proud degree know as farmer's gratification.

Kryo has become a mortal ingredient; one with the earth so to speak, as his hands and feet replaced the earth around the farmland. The more he unearthed and replenished the soils, the deeper the connection grew that he was impulsive abut earlier.

It was as if; he had that very outlined prospective Mr. Levi had when he worked back and forth the narrow passages of the crop beds.

Kyro slowly buy consciously understood *the mythology of»» never question mother earth, Mother Nature and the mother of all irony* all too well— because it was transmitted through the textile of the earth that has been passing through his fingertips.

Kyro was caring for the fruitless trees as if he was attending to a replication of his very being; he was kind, thoughtful, diligent and generous with his manoeuvre... as he went from one end to the others.

Mustave was also immaculate at performing the redistribution of fresh earth symphony.

The mood on mount-7 has never been this cereal; just like the days when Mr. Levi was alive.

The playful camaraderie of Kyro and Mustave restoring the earth around the fruitless trees, resonated in laughter... as their friendship took to the skies; it went to highest levels yet on the farmland, on top of mount-7– which caused the mist to brows on the playful bonding that was happening below their guarding duties.

No one has yet to notice, that the strong empty rumbles that came from the pit of Konrads' belly, has caused him to stealthily depart from the visions of Mustave and Kyro.

Konrad has finally gotten that moment, that opportunity he'd been feigning, ever since Edith had placed his portion; of fried-fish, pudding, banana, mangoes, hard-dough-bread and sugar-doused-lemonade into the confines, care and controls of Mustaves' lunchbox counted years ago.

Without any observations or known inklings, Mustave and Kryo maintained their farmers focus on the process of restoring vitality around the roots of the fruitless trees... as the furry jackass Konrad, made off with the lunchbox— still neatly tucked away in his hamper.

Konrad was giggling with accomplishments, confidence and excitements. In addition, a taste of good appetite and the delicacy of edits lunch menu linger into his excitements.

It was evident, today was the day of repayment for all that Mustave had put Konrad through. Konrad could not maintain his innocence's any longer; he blissfully bursts out into laughter, "bahahahaha— Not only will he learn to share– but today hunger will also teach that glutton Mustave a wonderful lesson."

The furry jackass Konrad was having a blast, laughing at his previous hungry pains– as he kept sniffing the hamper on his shoulders.

"If this feast taste as good as it smells, I might just eat the lemonade jar and the lunchbox– to delete any and all evidences... not to mention, I might just have to devour my hamper, bahahahaha... he grinned... dam, he-ooon, he-ooon, this shit smells so good! Oh am I in for a treat today!"

Konrad was visibly impaired from the detection of Kyro and Mustave— as he sought a secure location far-away from the two.

Konrad relied on his consciences and hunger to guide him and his hamper in the perfect location, a measurable distance away from Kyro and his gluttonous friend Mustave.

Konrad sat down under the comforts of two shaded trees; before Konrad sat down, he stretched his mussels and yawned everlastingly.

Finally seated with eyes and hoofs on his prize, Konrad opened the lunchbox and began marvelling in the smell of his lunch. Konrad then closed his eyes and remembers the times he was punished by Mustave. He then took out one of the fried-fish, kissed it on its forehead and immediately tossed it into his mouth... jewelling with reliefs, Konrad used a slice of hard-dough-brad to wipe the corners of his mouth.

"Em, em, em, Edith has got to open a jackass canteen for me and my jackass companions... eating grass is exactly what is it– eating grass; now, fried-fish, hard-dough-bread, pudding and sugar-doused-lemonade takes on a completely new meaning... it will make honest jackass such as myself, stoop to a thieves level.

This is hoof licking and tail wagging good. I hope, I do not fall asleep like that glutton Mustave"... laughter conspired around the feast– as Konrad made the best of both slices of pudding.

Konrad was one step closer to the understanding of why Mustave has been so selfish with both portions of the lunch menu.

He was beginning to feel a bit of pity for him as well; but as he held the lemonade jar right side-up at his head, all that sense of pity washed into his belly, naturally the same way as the fried-fishes, pudding and hard-dough-brad has done.

All that was left in the lunchbox were 2 bananas and 2 whole ripe mangoes, so Konrad discarded the fruits into the bushes because he'd already had his shares of banana leaves and mango leaves and they too tasted like grass.

Konrad was full to the brim! He found that just after he gobbled the jar of sugar-doused-lemonade, he was beginning to drift from conscious into a coma-toasts state of: mind and body relaxations. Basically he was already falling asleep and he knew what the circumstances of sleep on duty could manifest into; an ass whopping, if he was caught by Mustave.

"Snap out of it" said Konrad. He shook his head and then wiggled his oversize-ears but that did little justice. Konrad wobbles to his feet, with his ears stuck to his neck from the momentary nap that he was under.

Konrad was reeking with the smell of lunch that Edith had prepared to share– as he fought tremendously to rid himself of a sense of over-comfort that was quickly leading him on his side; to commence his afternoon nap.

However, the sound of Mustaves' distressing cries and calls implemented a sense of urgency, to literally snap the hell of his lunch anaesthesia.

Konrad could taste the anger infused with deep hunger that came from the calls and cries of the tongue of Mustave. without a solution to his drama that was about to unfold; Konrad took off on all hoofing four cylinders, 100 miles an hour down the valley of shame.

Mustave was closing in on the crime scene– where Konrad sat and devoured both portions of the lunchbox. Kyro was laughing uncontrollably— as he watched the dilemma unfolding at a 100 miles an hour.

"This is way too funny" said Kyro.

Nonetheless, this was a serious matter for both Mustave and Konrad. Only the gods were able to predict what would happen to Konrad, if he was caught by Mustave; who demonstrated his hunger and explosive anger... as he tossed»» a handful of rocks at the head of his four-hoofed-transportation-Konrad. "Motherfucking jackass, I am going to kick the shit out of you!"

It was fair to say Mustave was beyond livid, beyond humane and suppressed beyond hungry. Konrad galloped as fast as he could but the 2 crispy fried-fishes, 2 slices of pudding, 1 jar of sugar-doused-lemonade and 4 slices of hard-dough-bread had already began to spread into his blood stream, which meant: laziness has secretly snuck up on him. Konrad was beginning to lose his stability, his strengths and speed.

Mustave was within his reach, permeated to give Konrad a proper ass beating.

As Konrad darted around a shrub-garden, the earth opened up and swallowed him whole. Mustave couldt not slow his speedy momentum quick enough and he too was overcome by the gaping hole in the ground.

Suddenly the situation went from intense; to the disappearance of Konrad and Mustave. Kyro saw what had happened and run as quickly as he could to access the situation but he was powerless to help.

Konrad and Mustave had fallen far beyond his reach.

Kyro shouted into the gaping hole empathetically. "Mustave" he called "are you alright?" He repeated his attempts. "Mustave are you down there?" But silence was all that evaluated his replies. Suddenly Kyro found himself feuding in a sense of phobia and panic.

20 minutes has passed— and yet there was still no sight or sound of either Konrad or Mustave.

It felt as if an elephant had taken control of the acres of mount-7.

"How could this have happened so suddenly?" Kyro questioned the deafening silence that pulsed through his mind and ears.

"I thought we were all here to distribute earth around the crop-beds? not to be chasing a jackass around for fried-fish, pudding and hard-dough-bread.

Maybe this will teach both of them the ultimate lessons; of what it truly means to share and I mean that sincerely.

How could a jackass be so greedy for fried-fish, pudding, banana, mangoes, lemonade and hard-dough-bread? I thought they are supposed to eat grass and hay?"

Nevertheless, Kyro was frantic and coaxed by fear.

"How am I to explain all of this; that a jackass ate his lunch and he chased his jackass into oblivion? We are going to be in more than jackass shit and trouble."

The thought of him venturing back into the village without his best friend Mustave and his jackass Konrad was like a dozen elephants sat upright in his pocket— it was a heavy load to carry... so Kyro thought that it will be best if he waited for Konrad and Mustave to signal that all was well.

Two-and-a-half hours have elapsed since the disappearance of Mustave and Konrad.

Kyro was getting ever more weary and concerned for the safety of Konrad and Mustave. There were no sounds or movements inside the wide open hole. The only thing that moved was the hour hand, the mist of mount-7 and the fast approaching darkness.

Low and behold, Edith was also moving up the hills of mount-7 at an impressive rate as if she knew something was beyond ordinary.

"I've got to pick up my paces" she utters. "It's almost dark and I've not yet prepared dinner for Mustave. I shore hope to find a few heads of lettuce, some potatoes, tomatoes and or melons. I just cannot let Mustave go to his bed without a bite to eat."

Edith took a sip of her water— as though she wanted to wash her worries at the bottom end of the digestive tracks.

All that kept replaying in her mind was a meal for Mustave. He was the most important part of her concerns and worries. "Another few minutes and I should be at the farming grounds... I only hope there is something waiting to be harvested or else; I would have wasted all this time for nothing."

As Edith came closer to the entrance way that led into the garden of fruits, vegetables and fruitless trees, there was a powerful beam of light that shines with a blinding gleam, Edith placed her hands across her eyes to shield the powerful gleam that grew brighter with each step she took closer into the farm land.

Edith's suspicions went on highest alert— because moments before, she could barely see; because dark was vastly approaching and to find a blinding gleam of light this powerful when the sun was already gone down: was an epidemic worthy of all her concerns.

This powerful beam of light was so bright; it led Edith to detect the freshly unearthed dirt that was placed around the fruitless trees between each crop bed.

It was rather puzzling– because no one should be up the mountain doing this sort of thing.

Suddenly that scary feeling and high concerns that she had moments before she saw fresh earth around the fruitless trees, taken hold of Edith.

Not only was the redistributed earth visibly-present, she clearly identified hoof imprints along with several sets of foot prints as well. Immediately Konrad and Mustave came to mind.

Nonetheless, she pushed that impulsive intuition aside– because it was highly possible but it should rather be impossible for Konrad and Mustave to be on the hills of mount-7 because Konrad and Mustave were not the type to sneak away from school.

However, she decided to call their names to settle her disturbed intuition. "Konrad, Mustave my love, are you two here?" she called and asked as her voice echoed across the plains of mount-7– then traveled into the ears of Kyro; who was patiently waiting at the edge of the open hole.

Kyro jumped to his feet quite surprised but riddled with a degree of fear as well. He was unsure if it was a good idea to reply to the echoed calls or pretend that it was just an illusion of his worries. However, the echoed called came into his domain once again, not only was he scared but equally relieved that someone has come to his aide.

Kyro replied. "Over here, I am just a yard or two away from the shrub growth."

Edith heard his replies and went in search of his voice but the replies she heard was neither of her jackass Konrad or Mustave; it was far beyond her recognitions, further more it was troubling than settling.

On the other hand, it was a short rejoicing moment for Kyro because the blinding gleam was overwhelming his visions intensely more than it did to Edith.

Kyro placed his hands above his eyes to shield the bright powerful rays of gleams that were ascending upwards from deep within the hole inside the ground.

An ominous elusion he wondered, how did the sun ended up in this hole?

...What Kyro thought was the sun was something that has journeyed from the Mayans reservation campgrounds, far beyond the shores of the village.

Around the plains and valleys of mount-7 the quickly approaching darkness had settled dominantly still upon the livelihood of all things present.

No longer were the shadows of the late evening visible, the branches of the trees and shrubs gardens had settled as if a presence had captured their attention. The mist of mount-7 had shifted their guard and went in search of the cries of Kyro as he stood with his hand shielding his vision. Strange noises began to ascend with the blinding gleam but the sad news was that; these noises did not resemble any replies of Konrad or Mustave.

This intriguing collage of noises got louder as if it was about to break the surface at any moment's notice.

The earth began to tremble uncontrollably under the bottom of the foot of Kyro, distressingly so; Kyro lost his balance and feel backwards.

He quickly regained his stature. What Kyro beheld in his vision when he stood firm was a meaningful mystery he'd never forget.

At the center of the blinding gleam of light; stood his best friend Mustave and his jackass Konrad— with his hampers full of»» ***Golden-Nuggets...***

Interestingly enough, Mustave and Konrad were not alone.

The blinding source of light was housed inside a sailor's lantern that was perched on top of the wheelhouse, just a few feet from where a shipper's anchor resided.

The letters that were etched into the vessel reads: ***The Spaniard» Servant» Of the Seas.***

Her deck and fish-pots were astounded with a ship load of ***Gold***. The golden reflections were magnified by the source of the light that was coming from the powerful Mayan crystal skull.

When Edith finally made her way to the gaping hole in the ground, she threw her water bottle away in regards to what her eyes had settled upon; standing beside Mustave was a figure she'd recognised all too well. Edith was speechless and so was he... Melvin ran to Edith and wrapped his being around her everlastingly.

Konrad and Mustave stepped down from off the stern of the Spaniard and walked up to Kyro. Mustave then pointed to Joshua and said to kyro... "Your father awaits your greetings on the deck of the Spaniard." "In addition," said Mustave "you were right about something my wise friend; there were plenty more here to discover and I think we've fallen to its discoveries.

Our fruitless trees, on our land, have produced acres on acres of solid *Gold*.

We have a lot of»»»*Gold*«««unearthing left to do."

"All this *Gold* that your eyes behold»» was only one root of reaped fruitless tree."

The moral of the story is: Sometimes, we will and have-found ourselves in the position of Mustave and Konrad, Mr. Levi, Edith, the Dubwises,' Mr. Mayor and Kyor.

There is a jackass like Konrad in all of us; stubborn and relentless to repay negativity that has been dealt to us.

In all honesty, we simply want what is meaningful and what is just— our own portions of fair shares.

In contrary to the facts; we can also identify with the Mustave that hides behind our selfishness…

We are all farmers that have sewn a seed in some way or another; it is not a given that what we planted will be reaped by us individually—but the implication of time chosen…

There is much to be learned from the dynamic creations of nature, for example the prettiest petals of Roses are grown on the vines of Thorns.

We should be a lot more conscious about the things that are visible and them that aren't.

We should not only place a value at visible surfaces—but however, we must always remember to search the circumstances that are hidden within— away from what is soundly visible-nature.

If we sometimes dig deep enough, we may find precious priceless gems…

Patients are a valuable virtue.

This book is a tribute to our ancestors, those of Egyptian decent; who possessed divine knowledge, mystical magic, the gift of foresight and wisdoms' beyond our own.

In addition, I would like to commemorate the legacies of: Nostradamus & the Mayans, for paving and painting intelligence into our past, present and further futures.

Contact info: superstar-m@hotmail.com

Twitter: @djusha

Facebook: @Kamow Buchanan